INES JOHNSON

Edited by Dragonfly Editing
Cover design by Yocla Designs
Interior Text Design by N. S. Seneb

Manufactured in the United States of America
First Edition February 2015

ISBN: 0990922839

Dedication

For Lynn Marie, my first storyteller

...and because after you passed, I found that box under your bed!

PART ONE

CHAPTER ONE

CHANYN'S HEART POUNDED RAPID FIRE, like the percussion of a woodpecker's beak, as she glanced up at what opportunity brought to her door. Two men stalked into her home.

In all her twenty years, she'd never seen a man in the flesh. The unexpected guests could be her salvation. Or they could cause her serious harm. Crouched behind a shelf, Chanyn watched the two figures thumb through her belongings.

Just an hour ago, the sound of their conveyance startled her from her work in the garden. Their solar car glided over the city limits and parked on her street. Diesel cars and trucks littered the decayed streets of the city, but none of the centuries old relics were remotely operational. It marked the third time a solar car skirted the edges of the city. The first occurrence happened when she was seven years old, the second, shortly after her fourteenth birthday. Each time, the protective windows of the conveyances had been up, and Chanyn, too far away to see in any case, couldn't glimpse the occupants inside. Neither of those two cars ventured into the deserted city. Why would they? No one would want to try to survive in these ruins.

The two men had opened the doors and disembarked from the vehicle. From the rooftops of the city, Chanyn tracked the men. To her utter surprise, they wandered around for a quarter of an hour before making purposeful progress towards her home.

Trying the door and finding it locked, one male climbed in through a window. A moment later, he let the second one in through the door.

Chanyn climbed down from the roof and let herself into her now occupied home. There had never been more than two people inside her home in all her life, and never any males.

Her mind told her she should be afraid. Men, her mother taught her, were dangerous creatures. But Chanyn's jammering heartbeat slowed as she watched the two males skim through the pages of her mother's beloved texts.

The first one, the window prowler, stood taller and broader than his partner, his skin the deep brown of the fertile earth. His broad shoulders strained the cotton shirt that clung to his back. Chanyn saw each movement of his muscled bicep as he pinched the pages, and then long, capable fingers followed each piece of parchment down as he perused the words. The oddly sensual movement awakened something deep inside Chanyn. The man's eyes, the cloudless blue of the sky, kept looking up and peering around. They had narrowed on a spot near Chanyn's hiding place, twice now; looking directly at the shelf behind which she'd concealed herself.

Certain he could sense her presence, Chanyn held her breath. But each time she thought she'd been caught, his attention was drawn back to the book in his hand.

"This is a waste of time, Khi."

Chanyn's attention switched to the other man. Her breath caught and she shoved her fist into her mouth to quiet herself.

"We're not going to find anything in here," the second man continued.

His voice was what Chanyn imagined music sounded like. The tone reverberated through her body and left her senses humming. But it was his face that made her heartbeat speed up to a woodpecker's tempo once more. He was golden. Just like the man on the covers of her romance novels. A golden mane of hair radiated from his head, like the rays of the sun. His eyes were light, like his companion's, but not blue. From this distance, Chanyn couldn't quite tell which color. Maybe green? Maybe golden? Whatever their color, Chanyn clearly saw the sadness in them. It mirrored the downcast lines of his lips.

To be sure, the man wasn't frowning; his face seemed incapable of the scowl required for the expression. Chanyn was an expert on the frown. It was the only expression her mother wore. It came in a myriad of minor quirks of the lips.

There was the Chanyn-I-can't-believe-you-don't-understand-this-simple-concept frown.

Or the Chanyn-please-calm-your-excitement-over-the-colors-in-a-flower frown.

"I'm not giving up," said the other man, Khi. "I'm never going to give up, Dain."

Khi turned from Dain and grabbed another book off the shelf.

That's when Chanyn noticed that the men stood in the reference section of her home. Specifically the medical reference section. All these tomes contained information of chemical and procedural remedies from the twenty-first century. Ancient prescriptions no longer used, all these centuries after The Great Destruction. The section was small. Only a select few titles had been copied from the brittle, wood-based paper of the twentieth century onto the durable, alkaline-based materials that could last for centuries.

Dain walked over to Khi. Chanyn could see that Dain, who still would easily tower over her, was perhaps an inch shorter than Khi, and a degree less broad. Dain's hand came to rest on Khi's shoulder, another hand on Khi's hip. It brought to Chanyn's mind the dance called the waltz. In the novels she read, of times long past, men would dance with women at arm's length, and twirl them around the room in circles. This is how the two men looked, but in reverse as they were front to back.

Dain leaned in to speak quietly to Khi. Khi wore a determined scowl on his face as he continued to peruse the books.

"Khial," Dain said softly in that lyrical voice of his, but loudly enough for Chanyn to hear. "This is one fight you can't protect me from."

Khial pinched another page, muscles tense.

Dain rested his golden head against the back of Khial's shoulder. The spun gold making a lovely contrast against the rich brown.

Khial's deep voice, when he spoke, was matter-of-fact. It betrayed the emotion on his face. "I'm not giving up on you, Dain. I'll find it. Then I'll make you take it. And you will like it."

Dain chuckled at that, a light rumble rolled across the back of his shoulders.

Chanyn saw Khial's face. She saw through the young man's bravado. Whatever was wrong, it affected Khial deeply. These men clearly had come here searching for help. Specifically, for information. Chanyn had grown up in the stacks of these books. If there was anything her mother taught her well, it was to find information. If she helped them with their salvation, perhaps they'd help her with her own.

Decision made, Chanyn rose from her hiding spot. Before she could make her approach, a loud squeal cracked the air.

The men had left the barred door open to the outside wild. Every human head turned to the entrance as a wild boar charged into the room.

Before Chanyn could move, Khial shoved Dain behind him, then grabbed a chair and swung it at the boar. The flimsy plastic made contact, but it was flimsy plastic, and only served to irritate the large animal.

The boar charged, its horned snout catching Khial in the thigh. Blood spilled. Khial went down to a knee. The boar retreated.

Khial clutched his bleeding leg looking up at the boar, now on eye level.

The animal grunted. Khial did the same, a murderous look in both animal and man's eyes.

Dain stood beside Khial, but Khial held him back with his forearm.

The boar charged.

Two gunshots rang through the air. The boar went down. Its head crashed not four feet from the men. Both men looked up at the direction of the gunshots and their eyes landed on Chanyn.

There was far more shock on the men's faces as they eyed her than when they'd faced the wild animal. Chanyn took this as her due, certain she appeared wilder than anything they'd seen in the ruins she lived in. She hadn't bothered to run a brush through her hair in days. Her leggings were caked with dirt from her morning tilling in the small garden out back. And in her hand, she held a weapon she knew was outlawed in the civilized city these men came from.

Chanyn lowered the firearm. Her aim hadn't been true and the boar squealed in agony. She put the gun in its holster and withdrew a dagger from her boot. An audible gasp escaped from Dain. His eyes -they were green by the way- opened wide at the sight of the blade.

Great! Chanyn had come face to face with the man of her dreams and, instead of swooning like a Victorian heroine, she'd dispatched of the danger herself. Completely emasculating not one, but two, men. Aw, well, at least she was now certain she faced no danger from these two males. And she didn't have to go out and hunt for tonight's dinner. It had been delivered.

Chanyn approached the boar. Khial's muscled forearms spread out protectively before Dain. She slowly dropped to her knees and plunged the dagger into the heart of the animal. Once the animal stopped clinging to life, Chanyn raised wary eyes to the men. Khial's forearm stayed stiff in front of Dain, his leg still oozing blood. Khial's eyes, though no longer suspicious, were clearly on guard. Of course they were; she was another wild animal.

Chanyn chanced a glance at the golden haired Dain, expecting more of the same.

What she saw caught her breath. Dain looked at her in awe, a slow beam of light glancing off his up-tilting lips and shinning across his face. His voice, when he spoke, brimmed with wonder.

"Are you an angel?" he asked.

Chanyn blinked. She opened her mouth, but to her utter horror and further embarrassment, only a grunt came out.

Khial narrowed his eyes at her, like she was a fool.

Dain's wonder dimmed.

Chanyn's shoulders slumped.

Her entire life her mother had called her a chatterbox and demanded quiet from her. If her mother had truly wanted quiet, she wouldn't have taught Chanyn to talk or read, and then brought her out into the middle of nowhere with no one but herself as company.

Chanyn tried to clear her throat, but it seized, and more unintelligible, unladylike, sounds emanated from her person. Her voice hadn't been used in months. And apparently, it had no intentions of working any time soon.

"She's just a girl, Dain." Khial's statement rang as an accusation. His blue eyes, when Chanyn met them, threw crystal daggers at her.

Chanyn recoiled.

But Dain continued to gape at her in wonder. She decided to focus on that glorious face that filled so many of her fantasies while she read at night, and daydreamed all morning. The sight of blood oozing from Khial's leg stole that intention away.

Chanyn reached into her side pouch, which contained a kit of bandages and healing ointments. When she reached towards Khial with the materials, he jerked from her, suspicion once more in his eyes.

Dain reached out his hands and took the materials from her. His soft fingers lingering on her rough skin as he did. "I thank you for this," he said in that quiet, lyrical voice of his.

Chanyn's lips still wouldn't let out sound but they did rise in a smile.

Dain mirrored the movement.

Khial sat up, the movement causing Dain's attention to break from Chanyn and travel back to him. Dain made quick work of Khial's injuries, while Chanyn knelt nearby, helpless.

The damsel in distress didn't work for her. Neither did the nursemaid. Having no way of impressing the men with her missing gift of gab, Chanyn decided she could take a clue from the heroines of her twentieth century romance novels and prepare the meal. Food was the way to a man's heart; she'd read that over and over again.

Chanyn took her dagger and began skinning the boar.

"What's a female doing out in the Wasted Lands, alone?" Dain asked. His eyes queried Chanyn as he tightened the bandage on Khial's leg. The blood didn't seep through the bandage, a good indication that the wound would close and heal quickly.

When he finished, Dain came closer to Chanyn as her knife made steady work of the skin on the boar's hide.

Dain reached his hand out for the knife. "This is no work for a woman."

Startled, Chanyn glanced up. This had always been her job. Hunting fresh meat for her mother. Tending the garden. Preparing all the food. Scouting for supplies in the ruins. Her mother never once extended a hand to help.

Dain's eyes were both earnest and eager. Chanyn handed over her dagger. With strong hands, but clumsy fingers, Dain took up the skinning.

Chanyn watched the play of his muscled arms. They weren't as big or defined as Khial's, but they were lovely just the same.

"My name is Dain," he said.

"Dan," she repeated. The word came out rough on her ill-used tongue.

Dain looked up, joy etched into his sculpted face. "Yes, that's it. And that's Khial."

Though leery of the way her voice sounded, Chanyn tried the other man's name. "Kyle," she grumbled.

Dain let out a gleeful laugh and looked back at Khial. I taught it to talk, his grin said. Khial looked none too impressed.

"And you? What's your name," Dain asked.

Chanyn took a deep breath and told him her name.

"Shannon?" Dain tried.

Chanyn nodded liking the way her name sounded on his lyrical tongue. She wished she had more names, as women in her books did. First, middle, and last names. But last names denoted which patriarchal lineage you belonged to, and men no longer ruled the world.

"Are you here alone, Chanyn?"

"Yes," Chanyn nodded, enthused now that the power of speech had returned to her. Then she froze as she caught the glint of the dagger in Dain's hand.

Stupid girl, she chastised herself. She couldn't remember the story of the heroine who gave the big strong man, who just happened to have broken into her home, her dagger and then told him that she was all alone with no hope of rescue. No, she couldn't remember that story, because that heroine never lived to tell her tale.

Dain's hand stilled in its motion of slicing the boar's hide. The enthusiasm drained from his face as he watched her expression change.

"You know, Chanyn," he said. "I'm not as good at this as I thought." He turned the dagger around so that the blade faced his gut and the blunt handle faced her. "Perhaps you should take over once more."

Looking into transparent green eyes, Chanyn took the dagger back and began skinning once more. Dain continued his line of questioning.

"How did a woman come to be alone in these ruins?"

"I wasn't always alone. My mother was here with me."

"And she is no longer?"

"No. She is no longer."

Chanyn allowed the weight of those words to sink in. Her mother returned to the Goddess five months before. In the months since, Chanyn debated whether or not to leave the ruins. She possessed no conveyance. The vehicle she and her mother arrived in nearly two decades ago had long been defunct. Chanyn wasn't certain which direction to travel. Her mother would never tell her exactly where they were located, nor from which direction they had originated. Her mother had never wanted to go back and, while she lived, Chanyn had no choice in the matter.

"How is it that there are no men to protect or provide for you?" Dain asked.

Chanyn shrugged. Her mother had an absolute distaste for men and preferred to live in solitude than anywhere near the foul creatures.

All her life, Chanyn heard tales of the horrors of men. Men caused the wars that killed millions of people centuries ago. And worse, men upset the delicate balance of the ecosystem that put holes in the sky, caused the waters to rise, and brought on Mother Nature's wrath.

Everything was men's fault, Chanyn's mother insisted.

Chanyn spent much of her time in the non-fiction section of their home and learned the truth of much of her mother's words. Men did cause untold destruction on the world. Destruction, her mother told her, that it took women centuries to set right. But men hadn't always been that way. Men had been capable of great love.

At night, Chanyn would crack open novels from the fiction section, a section of their home her mother paid no attention to. Between the covers of those banned books, Chanyn learned different tales of men. Gallant men. Chivalric men. Alpha men. Beta men.

Chanyn looked up into Dain's kind eyes. He'd thought she was an angel. It was the way many of her romance novels began. The lovers would see each other from across a crowded room and there would be a spark.

That's what she was feeling now. A spark.

"Dain," Khial called from across the room. "The sun's going down. We'll need to be leaving soon."

Chanyn's heart sped up again, as though danger were approaching. "You can't leave," she protested. "It's not safe to travel at night." She pointed to the boar that was now relieved of its skin. She saw that the door remained opened.

Chanyn leaped up and closed the door, pulling the bar in place that locked it. It was for all their safety, of course.

She turned back and faced the men. "This beast was nothing compared to what's out there in the darkness."

Khial glared. But it wasn't his attention Chanyn was after. She looked to Dain.

"Thank you, Lady Chanyn. We are honored to have your hospitality and the safety of your domicile." Dain smiled.

Chanyn's heartbeat slowed and nearly came to a halt. The halt, she determined, was her heart skipping a beat.

CHAPTER TWO

KHIAL LOOKED AROUND AT THE female's idea of hospitality. Not even street boys lived in such squalor.

Tall metal fixtures lined the walls. Each fixture contained a shelf stuffed with hard-covered books. Khial had seen a few paper books before. His mother collected the artifacts.

The interior of the space was free of dirt, but everything looked near tatters. The curtains hung in doubles where you could see holes in one that the other covered. Near the back of the long room, shelves and doors were in a state of disrepair, barely hanging on hinges in some places. The rugs were worn. There were no solar panels, that Khial could see, and as the sun began to set, darkness ran its fingers up the wall of books.

The urchins that ran the streets of his home city, the boys who were thirds, fourths and beyond, had beds and clean sheets in government sponsored homes. The Sisterhood would have no less. But this female lived outside of civilization, away from any laws of sisterhood, or protection of men. If Khial were one to care, he would think it unconscionable.

Khial didn't have time to care. He had more important things on his mind.

He rose from the floor and put weight on his injured leg. He winced, but the pain was mild. It should have hurt more, but whatever salve the girl gave him lessened the pain considerably. Khial picked up the tube of ointment. "Neosporin," the tube read. He had never heard of such herbs. It looked ancient and was incased in plastics. It was the plastic that told him the herbal mixture was from a time long past. Perhaps he would find what he was looking for after all.

Khial went back to the reference shelves and commenced his search. Thumbing through the medical reference section, he found an array of manuscripts.

The Merck Manual of Diagnosis. Gray's Anatomy.

Across the room, Dain sat, looking fascinated by the girl as she stoked a fire inside a pit dug into the floor. Khial kept a wary eye on them both. Dain was the kind to bring strays home. Wounded birds, hungry dogs, traumatized schoolmates. Dain would look over the creatures with fascination, trying to figure out what ailed them, what was wrong, and how he could fix them. Dain grew up with no problems of his own, so the plights of others intrigued him, like putting together the scattered pieces of a puzzle.

The girl roasted the meat over the fire while Dain continued to question her.

"You've lived here all your life?"

The girl nodded.

"Just you and your mother? But now you're alone."

The girl glanced over to Khial and then back at Dain. "Is he your servant?" She spoke in a whispered tone, but Khial heard her clearly.

Dain's eyebrows rose in surprise, and then he grinned over at

Khial. The girl, eyes fixed on the meat, missed the salacious wink Dain aimed at Khial.

"It's just," the girl started and then swallowed, looking down at her hands. "I've read that people of darker skins were once enslaved by those of lighter skins."

Khial took a moment to survey the girl. Her skin was the smooth brown of an almond shell. She was pleasantly put together. For a female. She wasn't slight and frail like the pampered princesses of the city. Her limbs were strong, her curves full. Her hair, dark as coal, fell over her shoulders in a mix of braids and messy waves. But it was her eyes that struck him the most. They weren't a solid color so much as the liquid movement of brown, black and gold. If he looked at her long enough, Khial was certain she'd mesmerize him.

As if she'd heard his thoughts, she looked up at him and instantly he was held captive. In her liquid eyes, Khial saw longing, which was unfortunate for her because Khial was unwilling to provide for her. For her or any woman. For anyone, save Dain. But Khial couldn't communicate that fact. He was having trouble breaking away from the girl's molten gaze.

Dain's laughter broke the spell. "Khial is neither my slave nor my servant."

Khial rolled his eyes at the lie. Though the Sisterhood outlawed any practice of forced service hundreds of years ago, Khial had pledged, when they were just boys, to remain by Dain's side always. Dain pledged to do the same with him.

The girl looked at Dain with stars in her eyes. Khial had seen that look of desire many times before, in both women and men. Poor girl, thought Khial. Dain had his mother's beauty. Dain's mother, Darlyn, had used her looks and desirability to amass wealth for her family. Dain remained blissfully unaware of what his smile did to the human population.

Dain aimed that up-tilted weapon at Khial. Though not immune, Khial had years of practice at handling Dain and his smiles. He turned back to the books.

He was near the end of the section and still had not found anything close to what he sought. His frustration growing, a new section caught his eyes. Khial abandoned the medical reference section, his hands shaking at the trove of these new treasures.

The Arts and Entertainment section was small and easily overlooked. Khial pulled a thin booklet out. *Andrew Lloyd Weber Classics*, the book read.

"Women outlawed slavery in all its forms centuries ago," Dain said. "No one can force another to do anything they do not want."

Khial glanced up to see the girl's eyes draw at this, doubtful of Dain's words. Dain took her hand into his own. Khial's wonder at his find turned sour. He stashed the book into his pack and marched over to the cozy pair.

"Dain," his voice came out as a bark and the two of them jerked apart. "It's still light out. We can make it back if we leave now."

"Nonsense," Dain frowned. "The sun's nearly set and Chanyn has prepared this lovely meal for us."

Trust Dain to remember his impeccable manners in every situation. The meal was burnt, chewy, and mushy, all at the same time. They ate with their hands on plastic slats. Dain was lucky Khial humored him; they had perfectly good rations in the vehicle. Dain kept up his inquiry of the strange girl. Khial was largely uninterested in the conversation. But one thing niggled him.

"Where did you get the firearm?"

The girl startled at his voice, as though surprised to find Khial sitting there. "There's a dwelling called Walmart about two miles from here. All of the canned foods within are inedible and the electronic devices are useless. But I've made use of the weaponry."

She indicated the firearm in question and the dagger, restored to her boot. Her eyes once again connected with Khial's. It was a warning. Dain, she trusted, but Khial, she was still apprehensive about. She was smarter than Khial gave her credit.

"It's getting late," Khial said. "We should retire now so that we can get started at first light."

The girl's face fell at those words. Her arms came around herself, though it wasn't cold.

Dain's face mirrored hers, his hands reached out to rub her shoulder.

Khial barely stopped himself from rolling his eyes. He knew what would come for him when he and Dain were alone. But Khial had already formulated a plan to distract Dain.

"All right," the girl said. "You can use two of the Reading Rooms—"

"We only need one." Khial met her eyes again in challenge.

She frowned slightly, but nodded.

They all rose. The girl led. Khial took a step to follow, but was hit in the gut. Dain's tap didn't hurt. It served as a warning for Khial to mind his manners, a lesson Khial needed frequently. Dain's eyes narrowed on Khial. The message clear: Be nice. Khial shrugged and followed the girl.

The room she led them to had a sliding glass door and more shabby curtains with holes. The setting sun gave the room a bit of light. There was a worn mattress on the floor, with old sheets to cover it. Books lined each wall from floor to ceiling.

Khial peered at the titles. *The Holy Bible*. *The Evolution of Physics*. *The Diagnostic and Statistical Manual of Mental Disorders*.

The last title made Khial freeze in the doorway. Dain bumped into him from behind.

"This was my mother's room," the girl said as she went about straightening up the already tidy room.

Khial didn't respond, his eyes still on the book stack.

Dain squeezed past Khial and reached out a hand to the girl. "Lady Chanyn, we thank you again for your hospitality. We would not have survived this day without you."

Khial shook himself and looked away from the familiar title. He would not let memory drag him down tonight. He had work to do. A plan to enact, to save his oldest and most trusted friend from his overused sense of charity.

"I won't be far, if you need anything," the girl said. She moved passed Khial without looking at him, and then was gone.

Khial gave the curtains where she exited a good tug. He set his pack down next to the bed. Turning to Dain he began unbuttoning his shirt, waiting for Dain's first offense. It didn't take long.

"We're taking her with us."

Khial didn't answer. He freed himself of his shirt.

"The way she lives is unconscionable. A woman on her own. With no men to protect her, provide for her, or pleasure her."

Those were the three edicts of men in their society. The only things men were allowed to do any longer.

"And you plan to do that for her?" Khial asked as he undid the clasp on his pants.

The garment fell to the ground. Dain's gaze lingered on Khial's barely covered package before returning his green eyes to Khial's face. "She might be the answer to our prayers, Khi."

Khial stepped out of his pants and strode toward Dain. "I haven't sent up any prayers." He began unbuttoning Dain's shirt. "The Goddess can go fuck herself, for all I care."

"Khi."

Khial pulled Dain's opened shirt down his torso. Trapping Dain's arms in the garment, Khial pulled Dain into his chest. "If there's a way out of this, I will find it."

They stood nose to nose. Lips only a breath apart. Khial's eyes shone fiercely as he looked into Dain's. Dain's eyes, as they had been for too many months, dimmed in resignation. He rubbed the side of his face against Khial's, the day old stubble rough against Khial's cheek. Then Dain pulled away to peer into Khial's eyes.

"You know that I trust you with my life, Khi. But I need you to trust me, too."

Dain was the only person on the earth he trusted.

"If we can't find what we're looking for, she's the next best thing we have to a solution." Dain looked over his shoulder at the glass door where the girl had exited. "I really do believe she's an angel sent from the Goddess."

An angel? That got Khial's blood boiling. What female lived out in the middle of nowhere away from society? It was unnatural. The girl had to be up to something.

"Oh, my goddess," Dain laughed. "You're jealous."

Khial's answer was to shove Dain.

Undaunted, Dain reached up and caressed Khial's chin. "You are. It's adorable."

Khial slapped his hand away. Dain grabbed with the other. Khial maneuvered out of this grasp as well, but lost his footing. Dain guided them so that they both fell onto the mattress with a loud thunk. The men continued the struggle, but Dain's laughter left him at a disadvantage, and Khial quickly gained the upper hand, pinning Dain beneath him.

Dain gazed up at him, adoration in his green eyes. He reached his free hand up and cupped Khial's cheek, all struggle gone, his eyes turning thoughtful. "I've loved you for more than half my life."

Khial flinched at the word love.

As always, Dain ignored his reaction and increased the pressure and insistence of his caress. "Do you really think it possible for me to feel for anyone else what I feel for you?"

Dain asked the question in a serious tone. His head cocked as though exploring the query from all angles. Dain never demanded that Khial say those three little words. Khial would never say them, had never said them. Would never need to.

Dain pulled Khial's head down. Their kiss was brutal. Khial plunged his tongue into Dain's mouth and Dain allowed the claiming. As his tongue explored the familiar crevices, Khial's hands reached for Dain's pants and briefs.

Dain broke away from Khial's mouth. "How's your leg?"

Khial quirked an eyebrow. "The little witch's ointment relieved all the pain."

"She's not a witch," Dain protested.

Khial's hand found Dain's dick. "Stop talking about her."

Dain went mute as Khial's thumb dipped into the crevice at the head of his penis. Coming away with precum, Khial circled the head round and round until Dain arched off the mattress.

Satisfied that he had his lover's full attention, Khial scooted lower on the bed. Stopping his ministrations, Khial waited until Dain's eyes opened to figure out what happened to the pleasure. When Dain's eyes connected with Khial, Khial gave him a wicked grin before licking Dain's dick from base to tip.

A shudder traveled through Dain, exploding from his mouth in a growl, just as Khial reached the tip. With Dain's eyes hooded, but still avidly on his own, Khial planted a chaste kiss on the soft pink of Dain's dick head. And then, without warning or preamble, Khial dropped his head, and sunk his mouth down.

A deep growl burst from Dain's chest.

"Shh," Khial admonished. "Or you'll wake her and she'll want to join."

The thought of Chanyn's lush curves uncovered hit Khial in his gut. Though he was already hard from wanting Dain, the image of Chanyn spread out before him made his dick ramrod straight.

For a second, the desire knocked him off kilter and he stumbled off Dain's dick. Women had never aroused anything more than wariness and fear in Khial. He decided to chalk the errant thought up to the painkilling brew the girl put in his system. He shoved the idea, and the girl, out of his mind. After all, Khial had a pliable man in his bed to please. The only person he ever wanted beneath him, on top of him, inside him.

Khial straightened and discarded his briefs. He reached into his pack and quickly found the small bottle of oil. Rubbing some on himself, he placed his own dick at Dain's entrance. Dain wrapped his legs around Khial. Completely entwined, Khial entered Dain in one thrust.

Dain groaned, forgetting once more to keep his pleasure quiet, else the girl down the hall became curious, or worse, aroused.

On another thrust, Khial decided to reverse his position on loud lovemaking. The girl should know that they were a bonded pair. Dain was Khial's and Khial had no intention of sharing. With that thought, Khial increased the speed of his thrusts.

He'd made love to Dain hundreds of times. It never got old. Khial knew exactly how to bring his man to the heights of pleasure.

He'd studied Dain's smile for over a decade. Learned what kept the sadness away, what quieted the nightmares. How to heal Dain's one and only wound. Khial was a model student. Keeping up his thrusts,

Khial gave a firm hand to Dain's dick. A thrust of his hips. A pull of his hand.

Thrust. Pull.

Thrust. Pull.

In a matter of moments, Dain was close.

With that knowledge, Khial released his breath. He always held his breath until Dain's pleasure was eminent. Not until he was sure his lover was close would Khial spare a moment for his own release.

And so Khial began to thrust deeper, harder.

Dain reached up to Khial. Strong fingers caressed either side of Khial's face. Green eyes filled with passion and desire. Khial's breaths quickened, his heavy heart feeling light.

Dain came first. His body jerking and convulsing spurring Khial's own release; a release that took his breath and made his heart pound in his chest.

When the shaking calmed to tremors, Khial withdrew from Dain and collapsed beside him. Dain pulled Khial onto his chest, laying Khial's head at his heart. He peppered Khial with feather-light kisses on his brow.

It was Khial's intention to stay awake, to keep watch like a man was supposed to do for his mate. Protect them, after they pleasured them into bliss. But Khial couldn't keep his eyes open under Dain's caresses. The sound of Dain's heart beating strong, the best sound in the world, lulled Khial into a sense of security. Feeling protected, in moments Khial was asleep.

CHAPTER THREE

THE SOUND OF SOMETHING LARGE falling brought Chanyn from her room and back down the hall. In hindsight, she should've asked herself what she could've done that two large men couldn't handle. But then she'd remembered the boar that now filled her belly, and she hurried down the hall.

It was the groans of pleasure that stayed her hand on the glass door of her mother's former bedroom. Chanyn had never heard such sounds. She'd heard the pain of an animal clinging to life. She'd heard the angry cadence of her mother's voice when she'd found Chanyn reading romance novels, instead of the approved nonfiction-reading list. She'd even heard the cooing of baby animals as they played with their parents and siblings.

Pain, anger, and joy. None could compare to the guttural sound of pleasure and aching need that reverberated from the glass lined room.

Chanyn knelt down and peeked into one of the holes left by the tattered curtains. She'd often looked through this hole to spy on her mother on the days when the older woman became too engrossed in her books to leave her room. Chanyn knew from experience that entering without her mother's permission would get her an angry shout. So instead, Chanyn would peer in to make sure she saw the rise and fall of her mother's chest before going about her day.

When Chanyn peered through the hole this time, the two bodies inside were stark naked and definitely alive.

Khial's mouth hovered over Dain's... private parts. From his prone position, Dain watched the other man's head bob up and down, his eyes were hooded, his lips parted, his fingers caressing Khial's face in an encouraging motion.

Khial straightened and Chanyn saw both men's—she could barely even think the word—penises. Dain's long and pink, Khial's dark and thick. Khial plunged himself inside Dain and the two panted and moaned their way to ecstasy.

Chanyn felt herself growing warm, just like when she read the vivid love scenes in her novels. Only she'd never read of two men making love to one another. Of course, she knew it happened in this day and age. She knew that after the environmental, biochemical and finally, nuclear destruction wrought by men, that female births became scarce as Mother Nature closed her womb to mankind. Chanyn knew she had two fathers somewhere out in the world. Her mother rarely spoke of her mates, and never in a kind fashion. Chanyn knew they'd been turned out of her mother's home after conception. With their work done, there was no further need to keep them around.

Men were perverts, her mother insisted. They only wanted sex, and would draw a woman away from her true calling as a thinking, rational, sacred vessel. Women were a repository of knowledge, not semen, her mother would say. All women, thought her mother, would be best to leave the brutes to the judgment of the Goddess for their wicked ways.

Chanyn listened to her mother's words. She read the required texts.

But she'd also read books on the banned shelf of their home. Those books with their racy covers showed men embracing women. They told of chivalry and alpha males and true love.

Chanyn dreamed of that world. A world where a man looked at her with the intensity Khial gazed upon Dain. A world where a man caressed her body with the care that Dain showed Khial.

Chanyn panted along with the men as they both reached their climax. The ache between her thighs nearly unbearable, with the possibility of relief so close, separated from her only by cloth and glass.

She pressed her thighs together as Khial curled up on Dain's chest and fell asleep. Chanyn had slept alone her entire life. Her mother never once tucked her in, as she'd read in children's books. Or gave her a hug, like she read parents did, in the books in the young adult section of her home.

So, this is what love looked like; beautiful, peaceful.

What would it be like to be held? To be kissed? To feel that sense of security in another's arms?

As though he heard her heart's plea, Dain turned his head towards the glass. His eyes looked right at hers.

Chanyn gasped. Embarrassed, she jerked back.

But Dain continued to regard her with neither a smile nor a frown. One hand rested behind his own head to provide a cushion for himself, the fingers of the other hand played along the sleeping Khial's spine. Both men lay in their full glory on the mattress. Dain made no move to cover himself or his lover. He simply regarded Chanyn with an open expression that allowed her to look, as though asking her to... consider.

Chanyn's hand instinctively covered her pounding heart. She closed her eyes and rose from her place on the floor. On quiet feet, she made her way back to her room, in the darkness. The sun had set.

The moon gave her little light, but she knew the way like the back of her hand. Once in her room she sank down onto her mattress with eyes wide open. Her mind whirling as she tried to grab onto its myriad of thoughts. It should not have been so difficult. Her mother raised a rational thinker.

Earlier, she'd thought Dain took an interest in her. His encouraging smiles sparked hope in her chest. His amused laugh made her want. With all the attention he'd paid her, Chanyn thought perhaps Dain might be interested in her. And then, to see him in the thralls of passion with his lover...

Perhaps, Dain was simply setting her straight about with whom his interests lay?

Or perhaps, Dain wanted her to join them in the bed?

Chanyn hoped it was the latter idea. She saw no commitment ring on either of the men's fingers telling that they were bonded to a woman. Perhaps they were looking for one. If they were, Chanyn would volunteer in a heartbeat. It was everything she'd ever wanted. To be loved, and to give love in return.

The idea of being nestled inside that cocoon of love shared between not one, but two, men was more than Chanyn ever hoped for. She sent up a silent prayer to the Goddess, clinging to the dream as she drifted off to sleep.

In the morning, Chanyn woke with a start. She'd dreamed of running her fingers through sun-colored hair while strong brown fingers caressed her body. Her sheets were soaked, but her chest was full of hope.

Making her way downstairs, she saw that the men were already awake and dressed. Khial sat with his pack over his shoulder, glancing impatiently out the window. He looked up when she approached, his face closed. Chanyn remembered his face from the night before, so open and vulnerable as he'd taken his lover on the mattress. No look of wonder or love now, in his eyes, as his gaze slipped over her.

Chanyn's hope dissipated.

"Good morning, my lady. Did you sleep well?"

Chanyn turned to the dining area by the fire pit. They'd been in her garden. She saw a plate of berries and a few strips of yesterday's meat laid out for her. Towering over the offering was Dain's smiling face. He was dressed in a crisp white shirt that highlighted his tanned skin and golden locks.

"I hope you don't mind, but I took the liberty of making your first meal."

Dain held the plate out to her then pulled out her chair. Chanyn's knees went wobbly at the chivalric gesture.

"Thank you," she managed, as she sat down.

Dain rested a hand on her shoulder, giving her the same brilliant smile he'd been free with the other night. "It's my pleasure."

The twinkle in his eye made Chanyn's lips part.

"I'm surprised you could grow such a bounty out there, in your garden."

Chanyn popped a berry into her mouth and nodded. "It's receded some since my mother went to the Goddess."

Dain nodded in understanding. The ground was only fertile when women were present. Now that there was only one woman, Mother Nature only saw fit to provide for the one.

Dain brought a plate over to Khial. He brushed his lips against the other man's forehead. Khial accepted both the plate and the affection.

Chanyn tried to look away, but couldn't. Though she knew it was fruitless, the yearning in her held her eyes fast. Dain turned back to her. His eyes told her that he knew she'd watched him, both now and last night. What Chanyn couldn't figure was whether he mocked her solitude, or extended an invitation.

"We're leaving soon, Chanyn."

Chanyn's face fell. So that look last night had been to set her straight. He was in a bond with Khial, and there was no room, nor desire, for her.

"You deserve to be put up in the comfort and luxury for which your sex affords you." Dain glanced around the room.

It was the first time Chanyn had seen the man frown or look displeased. She looked around her home and tried to see it from his perspective. The crumbling paint on the wall. The dust that never went away. The worn furniture and dreariness of the ruined establishment. Suddenly she felt embarrassed by the way she lived, though she knew no other way.

"I cannot leave you here alone," Dain continued. "It would go against everything I believe in."

Chanyn nodded, a spark of hope lit her chest. At least they would take her with them. There would be other males in the city. Many more. She was sure to find love there. She just hoped they had the kind eyes and easy laugh of Dain.

"So, you'll come with us?" Dain looked surprised, as though he'd prepared more words to convince her.

Chanyn needed no convincing. She would never achieve her dreams here, alone. More than comfort or luxury, Chanyn wanted human companionship, love, and a family of her own. The city was the only place she would get that.

Dain came forward, his hands outstretched. Chanyn's heart sped up. She'd read about hugs. Saw couples embracing on paperbacks. Saw parents with their arms around children on hardbacks. She'd seen small squirrels wrestling each other over nuts, jumping on each other's back.

In her youth, Chanyn had watched the animals from up high in a tree. So rapt that when she leaned in for a closer look, she lost her balance and fell to the ground. She'd limped to her mother with a huge bruise on her leg, sniffling, she held her arms out. Her mother backed away from her as though she saw signs of the plague, and she'd told Chanyn to get busy with the first aid kit, and then get dinner ready.

Now, looking up at Dain, Chanyn held her breath with anticipation. But instead of an embrace, Dain clasped her shoulders with his big hands and squeezed. His face shone radiant as he looked at her. Chanyn's heart did another flip and she stared up into his lovely face.

"Pack your things, my lady. We will be in the city before nightfall."

Dain released her and began clearing away Chanyn's empty plate. When Chanyn glanced up, she met Khial's clear blue eyes. For all the joy Dain displayed, Khial looked none too pleased about this decision. His scowl reminded Chanyn of her mother's distaste when Chanyn tried to seek comfort after falling from a tree.

CHAPTER FOUR

FROM THE OUTSIDE LOOKING IN, Khial's childhood home resembled a palatial estate befitting his family's ancestry. But from the inside, looking out through a child's eyes, it could best be described as a jungle. A wild, treacherous place where one wrong turn could lead to eminent danger. An empty hall could quickly erupt with adults spewing hot words meant to scald anyone in their path. A man lying wounded in the corner was never a candidate for pity or help. A scar behind Khial's ear proved that. Most importantly, a woman's smile was never a good sign. It was a mirage that could lead to injury or death.

In the bright morning sun of the ruined city in the Wasted Lands, the dark haired girl came up beside Khial with a tattered bag slung over her shoulder, a crate of books in her hands, and the naive, trusting smile of a wild animal who'd never encountered mankind before. Khial glanced down at the books in the crate to see tanned men, some with long golden hair, others with dark waves about their faces. In each picture the men embraced a woman. The girl, noticing Khial's perusal of her reading selection, smiled shyly. Khial's blood went cold. He turned away from what his past told him was a trap and slid into the front seat of the conveyance.

With the car loaded, heavier by its new addition and the remnants of her solitary life, Khial had a decision to make. He could take the high road, turn on the hover craft capabilities of the car and sail safely through the skies back to the city. Or he could take the low road, which was actually a road. The old highway systems of what used to be called the States of North America. The intersecting tar pavements crossing the barren land were reduced to rubble in most spots, ending at collapsed bridges in others. The pathways were filled with roaming beasts such as lions, bears, and apes, which were once held captive in enclosures called zoos. It was a treacherous place, those wild lands, a jungle where men no longer roamed.

Khial peered up at the clear, cloudless sky. He turned the ignition, and pulled out onto the road.

It was Khial's first time out of the city. He'd wanted to see with his own eyes the ruins of man. Towers touched the sky with half of the face of the building gone. The land lay barren, dry. The few patches of green here and there was evidence of female animals who maintained the favor of the Goddess.

For the majority of the trip, Dain peppered the girl with questions about her origins, and how she came to be in the ruins. The girl only knew that her mother came from the city, the only remaining city on the northwestern continent. A few settlements remained in the southwestern hemisphere, where the land was more lush. The continent of Europa was nearly barren, as well as all of the northern Africas. That part of the world had been blown to bits by nuclear bombs and left mostly uninhabitable by the resulting radiation. The people who did survive fled to the islands of the Australias and Asia.

The girl chattered on, gazing at Dain with stars in her eyes. If the romance novels hadn't already decided Khial's mind about her, the stories the girl told of her mother confirmed Khial's conclusions. The girl's mother had been a female separatist, a small sect of women who believed the female gender were the chosen of the Goddess. Their aim was to complete Mother Nature's work by shutting out men from the cities and leaving them to their own devices to die out in the barren wilds of the earth. It was an illogical argument if you followed it to its conclusion: extinction. Khial did not argue it. He was happy to leave women to their own devices. So long as they left him to his.

It looked as though the girl's mother had been the only one of her sisterhood to put stock in the separatist beliefs and leave the city and its men. What the mother miscalculated was that fanaticism of the parent often leads the child in the opposite direction. Khial ran to the opposite end of his parents' ideologies, straight into Dain's arms. Straight into Dain's open home where laughter burst from each corner, and love flowed in abundance.

It appeared this girl ran from her mother's ideology as well, but more askew of it. Where her mother believed in the utter uselessness of men, the daughter, as it appeared from her reading fodder, believed men were meant to entwine themselves with women, inextricably, in the name of love. The problem was that she was trying to entwine herself into Khial's place of refuge.

The girl smiled demurely over her shoulder at Dain. As she turned, Khial's eyes caught the delicate curve of her neck. Fine hairs curled around her nape. The whimsy of those curls seemed out of place on a girl who felled and skinned a wild animal the day before. Khial's eyes dipped and met with the swell of one breast. She twisted in the seat and he saw the mound inside the flimsy cloth that barely covered her. The edge of a dark, brown nipple sent a shockwave to his dick and Khial lost control of the steering for a moment.

"You all right, Khi?" Dain asked from the back. "Do you need me to take over up there?"

Khial shook his head, eyes firmly on the road, hands gripping the wheel. No, Khial did not need his lover seated next to this temptress while he took a back seat.

They drove on in silence for some time. Dain dozed in the back. Khial kept one eye on his lover, looking for any signs of distress. When she wasn't gazing stupidly at Dain, the girl pressed her nose against the car window, awestruck at the devastation evident in the ruins of the previous society. A few times, both she and Khial leaned forward in unison to peer out the window at some wonder. Once, their shoulders met and she glanced at him with a small smile. Khial turned and spat out the window. She did not look at him again.

When Dain awakened sometime later, she gave all of her attention to him once more. Dain tried to bring Khial into their conversation, but Khial had no interest in getting to know the girl. His homespun mistrust of females aside, Khial knew the girl wouldn't be staying with them for much longer. So he grunted, shrugged, and then became mute, until Dain gave up.

By late afternoon, they'd reached the edges of the city.

The phallic skyscrapers and high-rises all fell in the Great Destruction. The domes that topped all structures of the surviving city rose no higher than two floors. Women believed that one must remain close to the earth. Solar panels, society's main power source, gleamed atop the domes, reminding Khial of a woman's tit. Steam rose in the air near the surrounding bodies of water, as an alternate to solar power. None of the cloying black soot from the use of coal and fossils of the 21st century remained on the outskirts of the city. No wires zigzagged across a skyline obscured by cell towers. Only radio communication and its short range waves were in use. Those waves only reached just beyond the borders of the city. There was little to no communication with other settlements outside the northern hemisphere.

Khial pulled up at the gates to the city. The peace officer glared when he saw a woman in the passenger seat. Women were far too precious to allow in harms' way, outside the city gates. Dain handed over his gold identification card and explained the situation, but the peace officer became more perturbed when he learned the girl had no identification, and was, in fact, being brought into the city for the first time.

By then, weary from the drive, Khial wanted to get home. He withdrew his platinum identification card and handed it over to the officer.

The officer did a double take. He turned, pointing at the platinum card. Two more sets of eyes peered over his shoulder, gaping at Khial. Khial felt Dain's tension expand from the back seat. Khial's nose stayed elevated. With a regal flick of his wrist, he motioned for his card. The officer obeyed, letting them pass without another word.

He could see the girl's look of surprise from the passenger seat. Apparently, she still clung to the racial stereotypes of the twentieth. He had no desire to explain himself or his status. After all, she would be departing from them shortly.

Khial navigated the clean city streets. Boys left the schoolyard after a day of learning. Young men gathered in fields for a few hours of sport before last meal. Grown men locked up storefronts and factories on their way home to their lovers.

That's all Khial wanted at this moment: a hot meal, a cool shower, and the feel of his lover's body beneath his own.

A young family strolled by. One father pushing a pram, the wife hanging on the arm of the other father. The baby's carriage was the green color of the earth, indicating that the child inside was a girl. Men and women on the street oohed and aahed from a distance. A look of deep affection passed between the child's parents. That look, some might call it love, was rare in triad bonds. But, so were baby girls.

When Khial pulled up to Dain's manse, he saw that they would not yet be afforded the simple luxuries he craved. But they would be getting rid of the girl sooner than he expected.

"Wait here," Dain placed a hand on the girl's shoulder before exiting the conveyance.

Khial saw the hostile figures in the archway. A bag slung over one shoulder, caught in the act of fleeing. Throughout the long drive, Khial had held his tongue, knowing this moment would come one day soon. The people on the step would put an end to the designs being drawn by both Dain and the girl, and Khial need do nothing but stand aside and soothe his lover after the fallout. He would be held blameless when Dain realized he'd have to part with his latest stray.

"Is everything all right?" the girl asked.

Khial glanced at her. Those liquid gold eyes threatened to pull him under once more. Dain had designs on keeping her. She had designs on staying. When she learned what lay behind Dain's family's wealth, she would be sure to run far away from them, along with the rest of polite society. Hell, when she met Dain's extended family and saw their greedy, hateful ways, she was likely to wake from the fantasy she'd dreamed up about Dain.

"Everything's just fine," Khial smiled. He heard the raised voices of the intruders from inside the car. A break every now and then meant Dain tried to reason with them, in his charitable way. Khial realized he probably didn't have to revise his plans of simple luxuries after all. He'd simply reverse the order. First, hold Dain against his body to comfort him. Then draw that bath for the both of them. And finally feed his lover in their bed.

Khial reached for the handle and got out of the car, sure that the girl would follow.

"We were so worried about you when we heard you'd gone into the Wasted Lands." Bil's voice dripped with false sincerity. Bil was flanked by his mate, Mikel, and their wife, Syndra. Bil and Mikel wore shirts from two seasons ago, while Syndra was dressed in today's finery.

"We thought you might not come back," Mikel's tone was laced with disappointment.

Khial saw the gleam of china sticking out of Mikel's bag. He saw Dain's eyes flick to the bag as well, but he said nothing. Dain turned a deferring smile on the older man.

"Thank you all, for your concern," Dain said. "Khial and I were just..." Dain hesitated, eyes glancing askew at the car and the figure still inside. "We were just curious to see the Wastelands. I'm sorry we worried you."

"Nonsense," Syndra came forward and placed a hand on Dain's shoulder.

Khial shuddered, and thought of the bath where he would scrub the poisonous mark from his lover's person.

Syndra continued, "There's no need to hide it any longer, Dain."

Dain stiffened under her touch.

"We know exactly what you were doing out there," Syndra said. Her hands paying undue attention to Dain's bicep. "We think you should turn over every stone in search of a cure."

"My wife is right, nephew," said Bil. "The thought of losing you is..." Bil put a hand to his chest.

All three, Bil, Syndra and Mikel, sighed. The sigh was not sad, it was full of anticipation. Bil was Dain's only living relative. When Dain passed on, Bil stood to inherit all Dain's wealth, as Dain's mother's only other living relative.

Just the thought kicked Khial in the gut: when Dain passed. It was the thing that kept Khial up at night. The thing that sent him into the Wastelands on a fool's journey. A fool to be sure, because he would do anything for Dain.

Dain was sick, and modern herbs and medicinals were having no effect. Khial had dragged Dain out to the Wastelands in search of outlawed chemical remedies of the twentieth and twenty-first centuries. But they'd come back empty handed. And the three grubbing bastards knew it. Khial clenched his fist. His body coiled, seeking release.

Just then, the car door opened and shut.

Bil, Syndra and Mikel visibly recoiled.

"What in the name of the Goddess is that?"

"I think it's a... girl."

Khial turned in time to see Chanyn shrink back just a bit. She ran one self-conscious hand over her disheveled hair, the other over her travel-worn dress. He saw nothing of the strong woman who'd fired between the eyes of a boar and then gutted it. Nothing of the woman who'd survived nearly two decades in the wild with only her cunning. Under the beady eyes of Bil, Syndra, and Mikel, she shrank down small.

Dain made a move toward Chanyn, but Khial beat him to her. He took a firm hold of the girl's elbow and guided her forward.

"This is Lady Chanyn," he presented her formally, as though they were in the courts of her novels. "She's come to stay with us."

Chanyn faltered a step as he led her forward, but Khial didn't miss a beat as he adeptly changed his plans. His hands clenched around her arm and brushed her shapely waist. Even through the layers of fabric, her flesh felt hot beneath his fingers.

Six fuming eyes turned to Dain. The bag of priceless china crashed down to the ground.

"You can't mean to..." stuttered Bil.

"But she's positively wild." Mikel took a step towards Chanyn. His path was immediately obstructed by Dain.

"A man who insults a lady, is no man at all."

Mikel recoiled as though Dain slapped him. Khial's fingers itched to do so. Though the law expressly forbade any man to harm a woman in any way, there was leeway when it came to harming another man. The consequences looked pretty good to Khial, at the moment.

"I bid you all goodnight and a safe journey back to your home." Their home was a one-story house they could barely afford. Syndra had expensive tastes, and no skills or political clout. Dain dismissed them and led Khial and Chanyn into his house.

"Who were those people?" Chanyn asked as Dain closed the door behind them.

Dain looked shamefaced when he answered. "My uncle, his mate, and their wife."

Dain walked over and once more took Chanyn by the hand. Khial's hands felt empty as he released her warm flesh.

"They are poor and rely on my generosity," Dain continued.

"It looked like they were stealing," Chanyn observed. "And they didn't appear to appreciate your generosity very much."

In spite of himself, Khial liked the indignation in Chanyn's voice. He could see that Dain liked it too, as he grinned down at her.

"Come, let's get you out of these travel clothes and into a bath. When you're done, last meal will be ready and waiting for you."

Khial groaned inwardly. There went his plans for the evening.

Dain walked Chanyn up the steps, where the household staff immediately enveloped her. The male staff of the house hadn't had a lady to care for since Dain's mother died. When Chanyn had been led away, with pampering instructions that the manservants took without question, Khial went over to Dain.

"She will be set upon by more of them," Khial said. Not just Dain's family, but her own, once they learned of her presence.

"And we will be there to protect her."

Khial scoffed. Tired, hungry, and horny, he finally opened his mouth to launch a formal protest.

"Take heed, Khial. We need her. She is our salvation."

Dain didn't stop to listen to the tirade that had built up inside of Khial. He went off down the hallway towards his office and disappeared around a corner. Khial watched him go with anxiety creeping up his spine.

He'd never been anxious in Dain's house. Never feared what might lie in wait behind a door or in a corner. After his fathers' murders, Dain had been Khial's salvation. After Dain's own parents were killed, he'd turned to Khial.

It chaffed now, that Dain sought salvation outside Khial's arms. It left a bitter taste in Khial's mouth that that salvation was in the form of a woman.

CHAPTER FIVE

CHANYN PEAKED INTO THE MIRROR, and a stranger gaped back at her. The stranger had the same dark hair, but hers was full of lustrous black shadows and deep brown highlights. The skin coloring was similar, but the stranger's glowed healthily; kissed by the sun instead of being burnt. The lips, full of awe, were a deep red and no longer cracked. Eyes, the same shifting liquid gold and brown, watched as those lips spread into a delighted smile at the reflection.

"Do you like, my lady?"

Three males stood behind her. Last night, Clent drew her a bath of the most sweet smelling scents. Then the large manservant, who resembled one of the wrestlers of Chanyn's sports books, led her to the softest, largest bed she'd ever seen. Chanyn climbed on board and fell asleep at once. Meaning only to nap before dinner, Chanyn missed the entire affair, awakening an hour ago when Tem roused her.

Tem, thin and wiry with large eyes like an owl, brought her to the sitting room adjoining her quarters, and tackled her hair. He painstakingly brushed each kink out, never once pulling or yanking.

Hurting a woman in any way was grounds for imprisonment.

And finally, Rianald, a shorter man with a slight pudge to his belly, dressed her in the most exquisite gown she'd ever seen. It was Rianald who asked for her approval.

The green material skated over her shoulders, drawing down into a V to highlight her full breasts. The wiring in the bodice supported and lifted her breasts. The material flared over her hips and backside before falling to the floor. High slits at each side revealed both her legs.

"The female form is living art," Rianald told her. "Art is meant to be displayed and enjoyed, not hidden and ignored."

Chanyn was definitely on display. She felt like a piece of art, the way the three man gazed at her. There was not a single leer in any of their eyes. They looked at her with a sense of pride in their work, mixed with reverence at her gender. Chanyn stood straighter, chin tilted higher.

"Do you think Dain will like it?" she asked.

Tem and Clent exchanged a glance, both of their lips lifted in smug grins.

"All men will fall at your feet, Lady Chanyn," Rianald answered.

Chanyn learned from the male servants that all females were given the title of Lady.

"In truth, my lady, we don't know what Lord Dain prefers in a female," said Tem.

Clent dabbed at Chanyn's cheek with a small brush. "He's never courted a lady in all the time that I've been here. And I've been here since before his mother's passing."

Chanyn's face fell. "So, he doesn't like women."

Clent paused in his brushing, brows drawn in. "Every man worships women. They are sacred."

"That's not what I mean," said Chanyn.

Now, Tem and Rianald mirrored Clent's look of incomprehension.

"I mean... well..." Chanyn decided to just come out with it. "He's gay. Isn't he?"

The men took their glances off Chanyn and looked at each other to see if one of them understood this strange, wild creature who remained an uncultured, ignorant thing, even after they painted over her rough canvas.

"Dain and Khial... they're... together." She felt her face heating.

"Right," Tem nodded, appearing glad they were speaking the same language again. "Lord Dain and Lord Khial are a bonded pair."

"So, maybe they aren't interested in having a female?"

The three men laughed at that.

"Every male pair bond, every individual man, dreams of having a woman," said Rianald.

Tem and Clent nodded.

"It's a dream that most men will never attain," Rianald continued.

"Especially thirds," said Tem.

"Thirds?" Chanyn asked.

"Third sons," Rianald answered. "Female births are rare since the Great Destruction. The majority of women have sons. First sons are first in line for female partners. Second sons rarely bond with a female. They typically go into trade, in service of women. And third sons..." Rianald shrugged and let the sentence trail off.

"Lord Dain and Lord Khial are first sons," said Clent.

First sons. So, that meant they were in line for a female.

Tem adjusted a fold in Chanyn's dress. "Lord Dain is very wealthy—"

"Very wealthy," Clent emphasized.

"And Lord Khial is very high born—"

"Very high born."

But then, "Why haven't they married a woman?" asked Chanyn.

Tem drew in a breath, but then abruptly shut his mouth.

Clent scrunched up his nose as though the words were having a struggle in his head. None came out.

Rianald looked at Chanyn, testing the weight of his words. "They've both had some family... difficulties that some women might find... hard to contend with."

The hair on the nape of Chanyn's neck perked up from its carefully brushed place. "What kind of family difficulties?"

Tem and Clent exchanged another look. She'd seen Dain and Khial do the same during the drive into the city. That look, Chanyn was coming to understand, belonged to a long mated couple.

Rianald didn't flinch from Chanyn's questioning eyes. His face softened into a smile. That smile let Chanyn know that whatever the "difficulties" experienced by Dain and Khial, all three menservants stood loyal behind their employers.

"That is information that you should hear from your bondmates," Rianald said.

Chanyn's heart sped up at the renewed idea of being a part of Dain and Khial's bond. But she shook her head. "They haven't asked me to be a part of their bond."

Now all three men smiled a knowing smile at her reflection.

"In that dress," said Clent.

"With that hair," said Tem.

"And that body," said Clent.

"You'll be spoken for before the third meal," Rianald finished.

Chanyn wasn't so sure. She thought back to Dain as he lay in her mother's bed tracing lazy circles on Khial's back while gazing openly at her. She thought of all the easy smiles, brief touches, and easy conversations they'd had in the span of a day. She thought of last night and how he came to her defense against his horrible uncle. Then she glanced once more at her own reflection.

Chanyn stood, spine straight, shoulders back, head up. "Where do you suppose I would find Lord Dain, right now?"

Rianald directed Chanyn toward the first floor, to a door at the end of the long hallway. She wobbled as she made her way down the stairs. Chanyn had seen pictures of heeled shoes. They looked lovely in the photographs and illustrations. They made her own strong legs look elegant and long. But she was sure the wobbling wasn't attractive.

Luckily, she didn't have to walk very far, and she didn't have to run any longer. Nothing chased her here. She was barely allowed to do much for herself. The manservants fetched her drinks before she noticed being parched. They brought her food before her stomach thought to grumble. When she'd had to use the restroom she was almost surprised they didn't insist on coming in behind her.

Women, they told her, were not meant to want for anything. Chanyn decided she enjoyed being an object of worship. She almost wished she had asked Rianald to be her walking stick as she made her way down the hall. But having been independent her whole life, Chanyn was determined to master the art of walking on the twigs of her new shoes.

She made slow progress.

As she got closer, Chanyn heard the most beautiful sounds emanating from the open door. Drawn by the sounds, she picked up her pace.

On the other side of the door, Chanyn caught the profile of Khial. His eyes were closed. His scowling face relaxed and vulnerable, like when he lay in Dain's arms after they made love. In one hand he held a curved instrument, in the other, a long stick.

No, it was called a bow. And the instrument was a violin. Chanyn had seen them in books, but she'd never heard the sound. The cries of the strings pierced Chanyn's heart and she wanted alternately to weep with joy and burst into a grin.

Khial appeared similarly affected. His eyes fluttered as he made the strings quiver. His lips would part when he pulled the bow long and drew out the sound. Chanyn couldn't decide what to watch. Khial's fingers or his face.

Finally, he pulled the bow to the end of its length and off the strings. He stood still for a long moment, until the vibrations fell silent. Chanyn felt trapped, feeling that she should escape such a private moment, but unable to move. She felt she'd caught him in the act of making love.

Again.

She remembered that when she'd caught them before, Dain welcomed her perusal.

"So, that's music," she said.

Khial stiffened. She expected him to turn toward her. Instead, he turned away and began putting his instrument away.

"That was the first time I've ever heard it," Chanyn continued.

It may have been her imagination, but she thought she saw Khial's ear quirk at that admission.

"It was better than I imagined," she said. "I'd imagined it was how souls would communicate, if our souls had their own language. No words of meaning, just sounds to make you feel what they are trying to convey."

She saw Khial visibly relax. His hands stopped in the act of putting his instrument away. His head cocked to hear her.

"That's probably a silly thought," she said. "You can't write music."

"Yes, you can," Khial finally spoke.

"Really? I've never seen a language for music."

Khial set the instrument down and grabbed some papers on a stand before him. Chanyn saw black sticks and circles written on the lined papers. She'd seen something like this before on the shelves of her home, but she'd never deciphered the language, assuming it was something very ancient.

Khial turned to her with papers in hand, his face open to her for the first time. Chanyn's heart sped up. Khial was a very handsome man. His brown forehead was high, calling to regal ancestry. His brows strong. His jawline sharp and angular. His lips so sensual when relaxed and not scowling.

Chanyn knew she stared, but she couldn't help herself. The thought of being mated to this man, having his powerful fingers on her body, those sensual lips on hers. She felt herself moistening between her legs.

And then Khial narrowed those aristocratic brows at her and frowned.

Chanyn crossed her exposed thighs, certain he could tell what was going on down there.

"What have they done to you?"

Chanyn jerked her head up. Her hands going across her chest, and then her middle. She didn't understand. Last night she'd looked like a dead skunk. She was sure she'd embarrassed both Dain and Khial in front of their family. Now she looked like the women they were accustomed to.

"Wh-what's wrong with me?" she asked.

Khial glared at her, his face, open and vulnerable less than a moment ago, now closed and locked with a scowl. He reached behind himself and set the papers back on the stand.

"There you are."

Dain's voice came from behind Chanyn and she turned, glad to be out from under Khial's scowl. When Dain saw her, he stopped in his tracks.

Chanyn ran a self-conscious hand over her hair and then crossed her arms in front of the exposed curves of her breasts. She wanted to cross her legs as well to hide her flesh within the slits.

Dain approached her and gently unwrapped her hands, pulling them from her breasts. "You look exquisite."

Chanyn let out a breath she hadn't realized she was holding. Her face split into a wide grin.

"They've made her look like your mother," said Khial. "That's sick, Dain."

Dain looked skyward as though calling for patience. "Ignore him. You look stunning," he told Chanyn. "And my mother was a stunning woman," Dain shot over his shoulder. He pointed to a portrait on the wall. "That's her there."

"That's your mother?"

The woman in the picture was indeed stunning. With golden hair, tanned skin and a seductive smile. She looked like the pictures of the heroines on the covers of Chanyn's novels. Chanyn couldn't imagine the family "difficulties" that could befall a woman like her.

"She was a pornographic actress," Dain said.

Chanyn's eyes widened. Even living out in the wild, she understood the implications of that title. Chanyn had seen books on pornography. Women splayed open for the enjoyment of men. Chanyn preferred reading her paperback novels to looking at the hardcover pictures. The women beneath the hardcovers always looked as though they were aping their pleasure; bodies alive but eyes dead.

Not Dain's mother. In the portrait, her eyes lit with joy and mischief, much like her son's.

"It's not a respected occupation," Dain said. "My mother's work made my family very wealthy, but she didn't do it for the money. She wanted to find a way to share her pleasure with the less fortunate. The men of the world who would never know the touch of a woman."

Dain paused and waited for Chanyn to turn to him. When she did, she noticed the defensive set to his jaw.

"She wasn't a whore," he said. "She only performed with my fathers."

Chanyn caught sight of Khial across the room. His brow raised in anticipation, as though waiting for her to make a mistake.

"She's very beautiful," Chanyn told Dain. Then she looked over at Khial whose brow lowered and scowl increased. "Thank you for the compliment," Chanyn told Khial.

Khial's head jerked back. She could've imagined it, but his scowling lips may have quirked up in the slightest hint of amusement.

"How long ago was this painted?" Chanyn asked.

"About a year before she died," said Dain.

"But she's so young."

"Yes," Dain nodded. "She died in an... accident. Along with both my fathers."

There was a slam and a loud click. Khial fastened the lock on his violin case. He turned without looking at either of them and left the room. The brief, warm camaraderie left with him.

When Chanyn turned her attention back to Dain his head was bowed, his eyes closed. A second passed. He raised his head and the dismayed look was gone. His eyes were bright, the brilliant smile in place once more.

"I wanted to discuss something with you, Lady Chanyn." Dain led her to a dainty sofa. "The decision to come here means that your life will change in many ways."

"It already has," Chanyn smoothed the material of her new dress as she sat.

"You do understand that women are scarce in the world. I know that your mother didn't agree with our ways, but you will be pressured to take a pair bond."

Chanyn nodded. Her heart speeding up once more.

It appeared that Dain misread her look. Concern etched his beautiful face and he took her hands in his. "Chanyn, no one will ever hurt you. It is not only sacrilege to hurt a female, it's illegal. There's nothing to fear."

"I'm not afraid. I don't want to be alone anymore. I *want* to be in a bond."

He smiled at this. "You are no longer alone. You will always have my friendship."

Chanyn's face fell. Rianald was wrong. Dain had no interest in her in that way.

"I promise that the choice of mates will be yours," he continued. "And I hope..." He paused, uncertain, looking down at their joined hands.

Chanyn got the impression of Dain as a child asking for permission to have something he didn't think he deserved, but was desperate for it anyway.

"I hope," he began again, "that you will consider Khial and myself for a—"

"Yes!"

Dain startled at her response, then he smiled. "Good. I had hoped..." He squeezed their hands together. "This is good."

Chanyn's heart thudded in her exposed chest. She was sure Dain could see it. He gazed into her eyes. Was this it? Was her first kiss going to happen now?

Dain rubbed his thumb back and forth over her hand. His eyes dipped to her lips. Chanyn parted them in invitation.

Dain brought his eyes back up to her face, his eyes widening more as he looked at the desire clearly written on Chanyn's face.

Dain disentangled their fingers and patted her knee. "This is really good news," he repeated and then rose. "I'll make the arrangements today." He walked over to the large desk that took up most of the room.

"Arrangements? For the marriage?"

He glanced up. "Oh no, no. Arrangements for your training."

"Training?"

"Of course. With a Pleasure Hound."

Chanyn looked on, dumbfounded. He talked of marriage and then was about to get her some kind of dog to train. "A dog would be lovely, I suppose."

Dain laughed. "A Pleasure Hound is a man trained in the art of pleasing a woman." He said it as though it were the most natural thing in the world.

Chanyn shook her head. "I still don't understand. Why would I need another man to..." To what exactly? Have sex with her?

Dain came back around from the desk and sat next to her once more. He reached for her hand.

"Chanyn," he began. His face now sheepish. "I've never... *been* with a woman before. I wouldn't know the first thing to do to please you."

"But shouldn't we, you know, figure that out together?"

Dain looked scandalized. He reeled back from her. "I would likely hurt you. A Pleasure Hound is trained to find out what pleases individual women. Then they teach the woman's bonded mates those particular techniques. It's an ancient tradition going back hundreds of years."

Chanyn still looked dubious.

"In our culture women rule. When we are bonded, everything that I have will essentially be yours."

Chanyn knew that in the twentieth century women fought for and earned a place in the government and the right to own many forms of business. But she hadn't a clue that the roles of men and women had shifted so completely on its axis in the past thousand years.

"Chanyn, on this one thing I must insist. I want what's best for you. In this one aspect of our life together, a hound will help me in achieving that."

Dain looked at her with such earnestness. In the two days that she'd known him, he'd done nothing but look out for her best interest. She supposed this was just one more of those times.

And so she decided she would try.

CHAPTER SIX

"COME NOW, JIAN. HOW LONG has it been since you've had a warm cunt on your rod?"

Jian shifted the packages in his hand as he walked along the paved way. The sun felt like a laser on his back, aiming right at his shoulder blades. A drop of water traveled down his spine. Jian ached to itch it away but his hands were too loaded down with the packages, necessary supplies for the Brotherhood, back at the temple.

"Unlike that little filly that got you in trouble all those years ago, I'm grown enough to know not to talk."

Lady Kathryn's conveyance sleeked down the street alongside Jian. Its conditioned air blowing out of the window, cooling him from the stifling heat. Jian glanced inside the car. A chilled drink awaited him in the passenger seat, along with ripe berries. He hadn't had berries in months. The temple could not afford such luxuries, and even in times when they could, his brothers felt it sacrilege to enjoy the fruit outside the presence of women, the divine creatures who made it possible for the earth to bear such divine treats.

"I'll pay you handsomely for your talents, monk."

Jian's eyes snapped to the older woman at the driver's panel. Though past her prime, Lady Kathryn was still lovely to behold. Silver at the roots of her hair, rouge to cover wrinkling skin, breasts lifted with the help of under wiring. She wore a deep pink chemise, the color of her own sacred fruit.

She'd armed herself in temptation, but the vile words that left her mouth turned Jian's spine to stone.

"I thank you for your attention, my lady. But the Code of the Brotherhood of the Pleasure Hounds binds me to tend to women only in the name of the Goddess." Not only did hounds exclusively serve women aiming to bear female children, they only served women in bonds, with the full knowledge and participation of their bonded mates. "If I'm not mistaken, you are past your breeding prime, and I do not see your mates about."

Lady Kathryn's face turned from serene seductress to scorned siren in a heart's beat. "Your Brotherhood is not long for the world as a result of your own lack of integrity, hound. Both your morals and your decrepit temple have holes. I won't offer mine, again."

She sped off, her wheels kicking dust up into Jian's face. He shifted the packages into one hand and, using his robes, wiped as much of the grime from his face as he could. He looked down at his robes and grimaced. The stain would not come out without detergent and soaps. Another luxury the Brotherhood could no longer afford.

Just as well. He had no clients to dress nicely for. With a sigh, Jian continued towards his beloved temple.

There were few people on the streets at midday. Most were at work or school. Two young ladies strolled arm in arm, their four mates walking at a distance. The two females snuck glances at Jian as they neared. The taller girl spoke behind her hand as the other one gaped at

Jian. When the tall girl pulled her hand away, the other shook her head in disbelief.

Jian could guess the trajectory of their gossip by that shake of disbelief. Young women no longer believed in the work of the Brotherhood. Myth, they called the female orgasm. Jian ached to tell them it was all too real and their sacred right to boot, but four sets of male eyes glared at him, and so he kept his mouth shut and his head down. Jian paused and bowed as the two women passed him. He kept his head down at the aggression of the four men who closed ranks around the women. They hadn't needed to. The Brotherhood was a pacifist brood by nature and creed.

The Sisterhood had long been leery of the Brotherhood of the Pleasure Hounds. Many of the older women had firsthand knowledge of the hounds' skills. They knew a single orgasm impaired a woman's judgment temporarily. Multiple orgasms, in which the hounds specialized, could render them entirely witless. That much power in a man's hands made the Sisterhood anxious. They need not have feared. The Brotherhood had no designs on earthly powers. Their order was entirely devoted to the Goddess. But one misstep in Jian's youth, one dark spot of misjudgment, brought the ancient temple to its knees.

Lady Kathryn's words echoed as the temple came into sight. There were holes in the temple. The Temple of the Brotherhood of Pleasure Hounds was indeed in bad shape. In its heyday, the temple had been a beacon of activity. Bonded triads lined up to use the services of the hounds, who had mastered time tested methods of producing female offspring. Even when unions produced male children, happy couples gladly paid tithes to the monks who showed the couples methods of bringing pleasure to all in the union, not just the females.

Now, without any females gracing their steps, the temple's gardens were all but bare. The domed roof needed repairs. The roof was work that a few young men could handle, but no young men remained inside the walls of the temple to accomplish it. Jian, who was in the last years of his twenties, was the youngest who remained.

He trudged up the walkway. Behind him, he heard the crunch of tires once more. Jian sighed. In truth, he ached for the feel of a female against his body. It was the greatest boon of being a hound. Being in the presence of that sacredness made him feel important; a part of the Goddess, a part of a family. Being of service, being needed, drove him to these doors after being discarded at a young age. It's why most of the hounds did their work. They were all discarded third or fourth sons.

That sense of being needed once clouded Jian's judgment when a young, newly bonded girl declared herself in love with him. Jian never imagined such a thing was possible, having the love of a woman. It had been a heady experience that he hadn't wanted to end.

Love was a rare thing, a divine gift, just like female babies. Gifts were not wasted on discards. Jian had been sourly disappointed by love. Five years later, he continued to pay the debt of that disappointment. What rankled was that his brothers were condemned to suffer alongside him.

Jian could take the money from women wanting only his pleasure services. That would fix the roof. Put berries in the bellies of the old hounds who still remained within. But Jian couldn't bring himself to do it. Giving pleasure outside of his vows was akin to expecting love. It would be a betrayal of the Goddess who had shown him a way to be useful, a way to be needed.

And so Jian turned around to face the stopped car with a spine of steel, to offer up his own dish of disappointment.

A man disembarked from the vehicle. A very beautiful man with golden hair, green eyes, and a friendly smile.

"Hello," the man said walking toward Jian. "Are you Brother Jian?"

"If you're looking for a gigolo, you need to continue down the road for about a mile. Place called Stallions. You can't miss it."

The man's eyes went wide, then transformed into an amused grin. "I'm not looking for male company. I'm in need of a Pleasure Hound."

Jian peered into the car. There were no others occupying the conveyance. "Hounds only work with bonded triads."

"Yes, I know. A female has just accepted my bond mate and myself."

Jian raised dubious eyebrows. This man looked a little too old to be newly mated. He knew the age and conjugal status of every female in the city. There were no unbonded females, of age, at present. Jian told the man so.

The man nodded his blonde head. "She's not from the city. It's rather... extraordinary circumstances."

Jian's hope sparked for a moment, until he remembered the chaos from the last time he trained an eighteen-year-old female just on the other side of puberty, but still not mature enough to be called a grown woman.

As though reading Jian's thoughts, or more likely being informed from the scandal, the man addressed Jian's concerns. "My lady is nearly twenty-one years and quite independent. She has lived outside of our culture and is not used to the ways of men. She needs help understanding me and my mate as much as we'll need help understanding her."

Training a grown woman with two devoted mates? Jian's interest peaked.

"I aim to do right by her, by blessing our union in the ancient ways that please the Goddess."

The man respected the ways of the temple? And...

"And of course I'm willing to pay a hefty sum for your services." The man's eyes skirted the crumbling face of the temple and then met Jian's once more.

Could this be the chance Jian prayed the Goddess for? A clearly wealthy patron, needing him to train a grown woman who was unlikely to harbor any of the childish unsanctioned fancies of love. It seemed too good to be true.

Jian put the packages down and stuck out his hand. "You have a deal."

The man clasped Jian's hand. "Excellent. My name is Dain. When can you start?"

CHAPTER SEVEN

CHANYN PLOPPED DOWN ON HER bed, finally kicking off the torturous heels. The plush mattress cushioned her decent and embraced her aching body. Chanyn's day had been exhausting. She'd been plucked and primed in the morning. Spent the afternoon touring the house and grounds with Dain. And then returned to her rooms to be plucked and primed again this evening. She never expected leisure to be so exhausting.

Instead of going to sleep, she had one more appointment to keep. Dain had hired the Pleasure Hound earlier in the day and his arrival was imminent. Rianald, Tem, and Clent dressed her in a sparse gown with a handful of ties down the front. It was the most reveling piece of clothing she'd ever seen. Not to mention, she wore it to meet a stranger who would help her perform intimate relations with the man of her dreams and his sulky lover.

Just two days ago, Chanyn had been alone. Today, she was trying to juggle three men.

She stood once more, too antsy to keep still. Dain had made no more overtures to her after his proposal. Instead, he started an inquiry into her parentage with only her mother's name to go on. It shouldn't be too hard to find them, he assured her. Women did not routinely run away from society.

During their time together in the afternoon, his touches had all been friendly, not proprietary. Their conversation had been as thought-provoking and engaging as their time in the car ride. They continued to learn more about each other and find things in common.

He hated beets. She loved them.

He loved the mornings. So did she.

He favored board games. She was eager to learn them.

He hadn't attempted to kiss her or embrace her.

Khial had been entirely absent the rest of the day.

"He's practicing his music," Dain answered when she queried the other man's whereabouts.

Chanyn ached to hear more of his music. She was sure she would get to, once they were truly bonded. Once they had an actual conversation without him scowling at her. Chanyn took her mind off Mister Tall, Dark, and Broody and waited for her carnal tutor to show up.

Panic set in.

What if this hound was unattractive? Dain compared the hound to a monk, that was like a priest. Most priests she'd read about were old men with white hair, pudgy bellies, and strict faces. Could she really be expected to have her first experience with an old, crotchety man?

A gentle rap sounded at the door.

Chanyn froze. She looked around for escape, but the only way out was the door.

The gentle rap sounded again.

"Lady Chanyn?"

The voice didn't sound old, it sounded gentle, pleasant.

"Yes?" Chanyn croaked.

The handle turned.

The door opened.

Chanyn gasped. "You're not old."

The man who stood in the doorway bowed his head. He was dressed in green and brown robes held together with a golden sash. His head was shaved bald, but Chanyn could tell that the hair that grew there was black. His coloring was a few shades lighter than her brown, darker than the tan of Dain's skin, with a healthy glow like Khial's.

The man rose and Chanyn caught sight of his face. His eyes were wide and slanted. Dark pupils peered back at her. Though they were dark, his eyes reminded Chanyn of a pool of still water. There was depth there that she felt pulled to.

He frowned. "Would you prefer someone older?"

It took Chanyn a moment to realize what he was referring to. Unable to pull her gaze away from his, she shook her head.

"My name is Jian. I am here to please you."

His voice reminded Chanyn of Khial's instrument, the language of souls. The tenor of his voice spoke of peace, serenity, and pleasure.

She tried out his name, "John."

He nodded. "May I come in, my lady?"

Chanyn nodded mutely. The hound came quietly into the room. He shut the door behind them and they were alone.

"Lord Dain said you were not from the city, my lady?"

Chanyn shook her head.

"Did they explain to you what I am? Why I'm here?"

Chanyn nodded. Great, she'd gone mute again.

She cleared her throat, determined to force words out and not be dumbstruck each time she came face to face with an attractive man. "We're going to have sex."

The monk's eyebrows rose. His smile held a hint of mischief, like Dain's when she said something naive. But, like Khial's, the monk's face was guarded as he regarded her.

"My task is to find what pleases you," Jian explained. "My religious order believes the Goddess only sees fit to bless a union with female children when the mother orgasms during conception. The female orgasm is an elusive event. Since women have become so scarce, men have little opportunity to practice their skills on women. Pleasure Hounds are trained in the carnal acts and understand how to bring women to orgasmic climax. It's my task to learn which triggers bring you to climax, and then teach them to your mates."

Chanyn gaped at the man, speechless.

"Do you understand?"

She nodded, mute once more.

"Do you consent?"

Chanyn forced air into her lungs. "It all sounds very reasonable."

Jian smiled then; a genuine smile. It lit his face up like the sun. "My aim is to make it pleasurable, my lady. Shall we begin?"

He reached his hand out to her. Chanyn took it. His fingers were long and strong, warm to the touch. Chanyn felt the warmth arrow through her.

"Will you pray with me, Lady Chanyn?"

Jian led her to kneel before the bed. Hands still clasped, he closed his eyes and began to speak in that melodic tone of souls.

"Maternal Goddess, I seek your presence as I align myself with one of your sacred daughters.

I offer my body as a vessel of your will and your grace.

The desire of my heart is pure and known to you.

I wish to please your daughter and garner your favor.

The miracle that pleases a woman and creates life is of your design,

Divine Goddess.

With great anticipation, I align all of the energy systems of my body, my soul, and my mind with you.

I give thanks in advance for your blessings of this experience, and know that I walk in the light of your sun, and the fertility of your earth.

Ashe."

The monk remained motionless for a moment, still holding her hands lightly. Chanyn felt energy humming between them.

She ceased to breathe while Jian recited his prayer. When he opened his eyes, she said. "I've never heard a prayer like that. Do you believe all of it?"

"Every word." Jian helped her rise to her feet. "Would you lie back please, Lady Chanyn."

Chanyn stiffened. Though she found this soft-spoken monk easy on the eyes and a delight to the ears, she wasn't quite ready to open her body to him. "What are you going to do to me?"

His still-water eyes pooled. "What I just promised the Goddess. I will please you."

Heat coursed through Chanyn's body. She glanced down at the bed and then back to Jian. He let go of her hands and took a seat on the bed, waiting patiently for her to follow suit. She sat down slowly, her heart racing. A throb arrowing between her legs.

"First I'll undress you," Jian reached his hand towards her.

Chanyn caught him by the wrist.

His eyes widened in surprise.

"I'm sorry," she said letting him go. "I'm just very nervous."

"You're also very strong." He smiled as he rubbed his wrist.

"I've never been naked in front of a man. I've never been naked in front of anyone. My mother did not approve of nudity."

Now that she'd found her voice, she couldn't stop talking.

"I have seen naked pictures before." Chanyn's face immediately heated.

Jian regarded her with those quiet eyes. There was no judgment there.

"I grew up in a library. I was surrounded by books. I know it sounds absurd."

Jian shook his head, apprising her anew. "No, it sounds like heaven. Books are my weakness. I began reading at the age of four."

"I began at three."

"What's your favorite book?"

Chanyn scrunched her nose. "I should say a classic or a religious text to try and impress you."

Jian smiled again, still no judgment in those deep eyes. "You need not bother to impress me. I'm here to serve you."

Chanyn shook her head, relaxing back against the headboard. "I'm not used to that: being served. I served my mother all my life. Now everyone is concerned about my happiness. Except Khial. I don't think he likes me."

"I've never met Lord Khial," Jian said. "But I can tell you that most men are frightened of women. Other men they understand. But women are a different species to them. Touching one of your sex is akin to touching the Goddess herself."

Now Chanyn regarded him. "Were you frightened the first time you touched a woman?"

Jian's mouth tilted in surprise. He leaned in conspiratorially. "I was terrified. I couldn't perform."

Chanyn laughed at this admission. A low chuckle rumbled out of Jian, a soft wave of sound as gentle as his speaking voice. And just like that, she relaxed.

"But that was very long ago, Lady Chanyn."

"Will you just call me Chanyn please? Lady is so formal and we're about to be... not so formal."

Jian bowed his head in acquiescence, "Chanyn."

It sounded different on his tongue without the Lady. Chanyn liked it.

"I will not harm you," Jian said. "If you feel uncomfortable at any moment, you need only say so and I will cease immediately."

She toed off her slippers and swung her feet onto the bed. Lying back onto the mattress, with shaky fingers, she began undoing the ties to her gown.

"My favorite book," she said pulling lose the tie at her collarbone, "is an ancient romance novel called *Flowers from the Storm.*" She reached the second tie below her breasts and pulled. "It's about a high born man and a religiously devout girl." The final tie rested just above her pubic bone. With trembling fingers that belied her steady voice, Chanyn pulled. "Against all the odds, the two fall in love and live happily ever after."

Chanyn laid her hands on the bed at her sides and glanced up. Jian was not looking at her body. He looked straight into her eyes. His jaw was tight, his expression unreadable. But in an instant his face transformed once more to the serene smile, his eyes guarded.

"May I touch you, Chanyn?"

Chanyn nodded.

Jian placed both hands at the sides of her face. With a featherlight touch, he raked his fingers over her eyes.

"Close your eyes, Chanyn."

She did, smiling as he continued using her name.

Jian touched her lightly, running his hands over her chin, her neck, down to her collarbone. He spread the gown wider. Chanyn felt a flush as she knew he was looking at her nude body. The flush held no hint of shame and her body arched into his roaming hands.

"You are very responsive, Chanyn."

Chanyn's eyes flew open. "Is that a bad thing?"

Jian tore his eyes from her breasts. "No," he smiled. "It makes my job that much easier."

Chanyn felt pleased at this. Jian went back to his manipulative perusal. Instead of closing her eyes, Chanyn watched his long fingers glance over her nipples. She saw her belly quaking at his touch. Her legs pressed together seeking friction. She heard herself panting.

Jian's fingers grazed her brown nipples once more. Chanyn arched of the bed. He placed a calming hand over her collarbone and stared down at her, waiting while her breathing calmed.

"I'm sorry." She gulped down lungful's of air. "I haven't been touched much in my life."

Jian smiled that nonjudgmental smile again. Then he stood.

Chanyn sat up. "No, please don't go."

"I'm not going anywhere," he soothed. His hands reached down for the yellow sash. With one tug his robes opened and fell to the ground.

Chanyn gaped at the display of muscle, sinew, and manhood before her eyes. Jian stood still and allowed her to look her fill. He was simply magnificent, but—

"You don't have any hair... down there."

"No," he smiled. "We learned that women do not like hair in certain places."

The bed dipped as he sat down once more.

Perhaps it was the light massage that he'd just given her, but Chanyn felt emboldened. "May I touch you?"

It was becoming a pattern that the men of this city all looked at her with raised eyebrows whenever she said something out of the ordinary.

Jian looked truly befuddled. "Whatever for?"

"Well... shouldn't I learn a man's body? I'm about to be mated with two of them." A concept Chanyn still hadn't worked out in her mind, but a fact nonetheless. "I've never touched a... penis."

Jian thought about this for a second. Finally, he lay back against the pillows and folded his hands behind his head. He nodded to Chanyn.

Chanyn scooted down the bed. Now that she sat before the appendage, she wasn't quite sure she would go ahead with it. But she wasn't a coward. So, she took him lightly in her hands. For all his peace and serenity, Jian let out a small gasp. Chanyn looked back up at him. The monk gulped down air and nodded for her to continue.

He was thick in her hands and long. She could not cover his length using both of her hands stacked.

The next thing she noticed, "It's softer than I expected."

It was also dry. She'd read often about the dollop of precum that would appear like a tear drop at the head of an aroused penis. Jian was definitely aroused, but dry as a bone. Chanyn was about to ask why when she noticed a purple ring at the base of his penis.

"What is that?"

"A contraceptive. It prevents pregnancy," Jian answered.

Chanyn hadn't even thought about contraception. In her novels, men often donned something called a French Letter, or condom, to protect from both disease and pregnancy.

As though reading her thoughts, Jian said, "Lord Dain has my medical documents. I carry no diseases."

Chanyn nodded. She went back to her ministrations.

She rubbed the head of his penis. Jian sucked in a shuddery breath. Chanyn looked up and smiled at him, pleased that she was having an effect. He released the breath on a sigh but said nothing.

She added the other hand and began a tentative massage. After a moment, Jian closed his eyes. She could see small shudders happening in his abdomen. She could hear his small intakes of breaths.

The sight of Khial bobbing up and down in Dain's lap, and Dain's eyes rolling back in ecstasy, came to mind. Chanyn dipped her head and gave Jian's penis a tentative lick.

The monk bolted up. Eyes wide, chest heaving.

Chanyn released him immediately. "What did I do wrong?"

It took Jian a full moment to find his voice. Finally, he shook his head, not meeting her eyes. "Women do not do that," he said.

"Why not?"

Jian's mouth worked but words didn't come out.

"I saw Dain and Khial doing it. Dain appeared to like it very much. If you're to train me, I want to learn how to do it well so that I can please him, too."

Jian shook his head from side to side, utterly flummoxed. "The pleasure of a man is not a woman's responsibility."

Chanyn's face fell. "You didn't like it."

"I... I..." Jian ran a hand over his bald head. "It's simply not done... by women."

"I think I'm safe in saying I'm not like the other women in this city. I'm about to enter the bond of two men who clearly love each other. I need to bring something to the table. You are tasked with finding my triggers. I already know one of theirs. Let me practice?"

Jian continued to gape at her.

Chanyn decided to take the matter into her own hands, literally, and grasped his penis once more. When he started to protest she was ready for him. "This pleases me."

The monk didn't stop her, but neither did he relax.

Chanyn leaned down and put her mouth on him once more. With one fluid movement, her lips reached nearly to the base of his penis and felt the cold of the contraceptive ring. She swirled her tongue around. Jian let out an explosive bit of air and his upper body fell back down onto the mattress. Chanyn continued her ministrations. He felt pleasant in her mouth. The rhythmic motions she achieved echoed the pulsing at her core, which ached to be filled with the same motions.

Above her, Chanyn felt Jian trembling. She remembered it hadn't taken Dain long to climax. What was she doing wrong?

She released Jian from her mouth with a pop and asked the question.

His eyes were glazed, his mouth askew. "Can't... Ring..."

Chanyn looked down at the purple ring clasped at the base of Jian's penis. She spied the release, and with his penis still in hand, she pressed it.

"Wait," shouted Jian.

The ring released and so did Jian.

"Oh, Goddess!" His body jerked as he came, and came, and came. Ribbons of his seed spread across his belly. Chanyn watched in fascination, as it seemed to go on and on forever. Finally, Jian's body collapsed back on the bed.

Chanyn felt very pleased with herself.

And then there was loud banging on her door.

Jian sat up right. "Oh, no. No, no, no, no."

The door opened. Khial stood on the other side, scowl in place. He spied the two of them on the bed. His clever eyes took in the scene and a slow smile spread across his face.

Jian dashed off the bed and grabbed his robes. He began putting them on hastily.

"Lord Dain would like a word," Khial said to Jian.

Jian nodded at Khial. Then he turned to Chanyn. Without looking her in the eye, Jian bowed and then was gone.

Khial chuckled after Jian as he left. Chanyn didn't know what was going on. She was about to ask when Khial turned back to her, mirth still in his eyes. But that mirth quickly dissipated. Chanyn was beginning to get whiplash from his mood swings.

His eyes roamed up and down her body, his nostrils flaring. It took Chanyn a moment to remember that she was completely nude. Her first instinct was to reach for her gown or the sheets to cover herself. Then she remembered; this was to be one of her husbands.

She sat there and let him look. It was evident from the way he shifted the lower half of his body that the sight of her naked was having an effect on him.

Khial's eyes finally reached hers, desire clearly written there. But then he shook himself, and a deeper scowl spread across his face. Without a word he stormed off, slamming the door and leaving Chanyn in even greater confusion.

She had one man she wanted desperately to kiss her, but he wouldn't take any liberties. There was another man who'd taken liberties, than leaped from her bed upon climax. And then there was a third who clearly wanted liberties, but appeared disgusted at the idea of taking any.

Chanyn flopped down once more on the bed, losing herself in the plush mattress, the only place she was sure to find any comfort tonight.

CHAPTER EIGHT

THE SOUND OF THE DOOR slamming reverberated through Khial's arm. He flexed the fingers of his right hand, clenching and releasing until feeling returned. It took a long time for the blood to flow back to his hand, it was still diverting to his dick.

Khial was sure the slamming of the door frightened Chanyn. He'd meant it to, to put some sense into her. What was she thinking, displaying herself to him like that? Showing him her rich brown skin, her firm breasts, her velvety dark nipples.

Her breasts beamed at him like the headlights of a car calling his attention. As she panted, they moved up and down with each breath. The movement drew his eyes to the planes of her abdomen. She was neither flat nor fat at the stomach. Her sculpted curves reminded him of the ocean. Waves cresting here and then there, going flat and then rising once more. Her narrow waist arrowed to the V between her legs. The dark curls like the rich black soil of the farmlands, the soil that bore the sweetest berries. He wondered if the richness there between her thighs mirrored the sweetness of a strawberry.

Khial picked up his pace away from the room. The scent of her arousal followed him down the hall. A woman's scent was an aphrodisiac to men. Khial had never gotten close enough to take a whiff. Now the smell filled his senses, making his mouth water and clouding his head.

For a second, back there, it looked as though she were about to part her thighs in invitation. It was an invitation he would never welcome. He slammed her door to slam the brakes on his desire and any intention she might harbor. More to shake up himself than her. As if he needed more proof that women were manipulative creatures who could end the life of any man who hungered after that place between their thighs.

This had to stop. She had to be made to leave, and sooner rather than later.

He hadn't argued too much when Dain wanted to bring the stray home. No creature under the Goddess deserved to live in such squalor and solitude as Chanyn subsisted.

Khial assumed Chanyn would run when she met Dain's conniving relatives. But she hadn't flinched. He assumed she'd recoil in disgust when she learned of Dain's parents' occupation. But she hadn't even blushed.

She was nothing like the girls they'd grown up with. The dainty, pampered princesses who wore their entitlement like a sash, and wouldn't lift a finger to wipe their own asses. A few tried to catch Dain's eye in their youth. For all Khial tried to protect Dain from his charitable self, Dain could spot a gold digger a mile away. Chanyn wasn't interested in Dain's wealth, of that Khial was sure. Chanyn was interested in the man's heart. In Khial's eyes, that was a far worse offense and a fruitless endeavor.

For all of the goodwill Dain bestowed on the world, his heart was slowly giving out. At this point, Dain was more interested in setting his affairs in order than he was in searching for a way to keep his heart beating. But Khial wasn't giving up. Agreeing to this scheme Dain planned with Chanyn was the exact equivalent of surrender. And Khial would not concede.

Khial had pledged his life to Dain's happiness. After what Khial's mother had done to Dain's family, he owed the man his very soul. Dain's heart was Khial's to care for and protect. Chanyn could not enter his bond with Dain. If Khial allowed it, it would mean that he had failed his bond mate.

Khial entered Dain's office where the monk, robes still slightly askew, stood with his head hung in shame.

"It is my fault," the monk said.

Dain looked the monk up and down, a small smile on his lips. The monk was a handsome specimen of male. Strong shoulders, large hands and a sensual mouth. Khial had never been sexually interested in another living soul besides Dain. But that didn't mean he was blind to the other man's appeal.

Dain held the contraceptive ring monitor in his hand. A small radio transmitter emitted a shrill warning sound when the monk's dick ring had been disengaged moments earlier. It was a device employed by parents of young girls in training with the hounds to ensure their inferior genes didn't accidentally spill into their daughters. As far as Khial knew, there had never been such an accident. Hounds were considered a trustworthy, devout, group of men.

Until recent history. Which is why Dain sent Khial to Chanyn's bedroom at the sound of the alarm.

"She's a curious woman, isn't she?" Dain tossed the device in the air and caught it with the same hand.

The monk stayed mute. His chin set.

Khial knew the Pleasure Hounds' compound was in desperate

need of the money Dain supplied them for Chanyn's training. The reputation of the hounds had been damaged because one monk ran away with some aristocrat's daughter. Since that incident, the First Sons wouldn't trust their precious few females to go under the tutelage of the sexually superior hounds.

The removal of a contraceptive ring was an offense of high magnitude. If a hound were to get a woman pregnant with his own seed, the Sisterhood would likely shut them down for good and persecute all the monks for crimes against women.

"She took the ring off, didn't she?" Dain's voice was coaxing.

The monk didn't answer, even though an accusation could mean he wouldn't get paid, or worse he could be brought up on charges.

Khial saw that the monk had no intention of selling Chanyn out. Khial leaned back against the fireplace, appraising the monk anew. Khial prized loyalty highest among all other traits in men.

"As I said, my Lord, the fault lies entirely with the teacher and his instruction," said the monk. "It might please you to know that Chan—that Lady Chanyn is very responsive. If my estimation is correct, and I believe it is, she is capable of orgasm."

Khial knew the monks believed that the female orgasm was necessary in order to conceive female children. Men had no trouble coming at the stroke of their cocks, but women, apparently, were not as fortunate. Hence the monks.

"We could forgo the one-on-one training," the monk continued, "and you and your mate can join us in the next session."

Dain glanced over the monk's shoulder and met Khial's eyes. Khial's heart sighed at the sudden stiffness in his lover's posture. Thank the Goddess! Dain wasn't ready for intimate relations with the girl. But just as Khial's heart breathed a sigh of relief, his dick hardened in anticipation of the time when they would partake in those relations.

Khial commenced clenching his hand once more.

Dain cleared his throat and pulled at his shirt's collar. A nervous gesture that Khial knew well. "In light of tonight's events, I would feel more comfortable if you took a bit more time in your evaluation of Lady Chanyn. She is untried and needs to understand the ways of men before we three bond."

From behind, Khial saw the monk's back stiffen beneath his robes. In the end, the monk bowed his head and turned to leave. As he neared the door, his eye caught Khial's. It was only a slight flick of his brow but Khial felt as if the man looked him over, sized him up, and found him wanting.

Before Khial could bristle at the evaluation, the monk was gone.

Now alone, Khial regarded his lover. Dain crossed his hands over his chest and leaned back in his chair stretching his neck. It was a catlike move that Khial had seen him do many times when he was stressed. Dain said the posture allowed his thoughts to turn upside down so that when he righted himself he came back with fresh ideas.

Khial always saw it as an opportunity to taste his lover's strong neck column. Bracing himself on the arms of Dain's chair Khial did just that. His tongue beginning at the base of Dain's throat and tracing a slow path to the underside of the other man's chin.

A low growl of pleasure sounded in Dain's throat.

Khial nipped at his chin before capturing Dain's bottom lip with his teeth.

"Hey," Dain breathed, looking into Khial's eyes.

"Mmmm," was Khial's answer as he crowded Dain in the chair and went seeking his earlobe.

"So," said Dain. "What did you see?"

Khial frowned as he pulled away. As he did, he also pulled Dain's shirttails from his trousers.

"Chanyn and the hound," Dain clarified. "What were they doing?"

Khial popped open a button on Dain's shirt. "You want to know the goings on in the bed of a man and *woman?*"

Dain's nod was a bit solemn. "We're going to have a woman in our bed soon, Khi."

Once again, Khial's dick jumped at the prospect. It was a thought and a feeling he was not willing to deal with, at the moment. Instead, he yanked Dain's face roughly to him and got lost in his lover's mouth. Pushing his tongue into Dain's mouth, Khial shoved all thoughts of Chanyn from his mind and tried his best to make Dain do the same.

It must have worked because soon Dain gripped the backs of Khial's thighs and pulled him down into the chair. Khial straddled his lap. Dain took over the kissing as Khial continued working on Dain's buttons.

But then Dain drew back sharply and grabbed his chest through the open shirt.

Khial hopped up. "Dain?"

Dain didn't answer. He gulped down lungful's of air.

Khial looked around in a panic. It had been a long time since Dain had had an episode. None of the medicinals the Physics gave him were working. Heart conditions were largely incurable.

Khial felt helpless as he sank to his knees before Dain. Khial's fingers clenched, digging into his palms, needing to tear at the thing causing Dain pain. Khial's own heart beat painfully as he watched his lover catch his breath.

Dain's breaths eased. His eyes relaxed and finally opened. With a careless flick of his hand and small grin, Dain waved the episode off.

"It's passed," Dain insisted bringing Khial's head back down for a kiss.

Khial stopped him, his own heart still beating wildly out of control. "We can go to the Australias. There are some old world doctors there who might be able to help."

Dain shook his head.

"You cannot ask me to give up on you." Khial was certain that if Dain's heart ever stopped beating, his would too. And Khial had a lot of living to do. Living with this man in front of him—this man who had been everything Khial needed in the darkest hours of his life. If he couldn't be the same for him, then what kind of man was he? He needed to do something.

In that uncanny knack of his, Dain read Khial's mind. "You want to do something about it? You want to help me?"

Dain waited for Khial to nod. Khial would do anything to save Dain. But as soon as Khial thought it, he recognized it for the trap it was.

"Agree to let Chanyn into the bond," said Dain. "It's the only way to keep me alive and you know it."

CHAPTER NINE

CHANYN PRESSED THE FOLDS OF her dress down. The light blue of the fabric made her skin glow a healthy brown. But when she glanced in the mirror of her changing room, she could see the curve of one breast. Chanyn's mother had hated any revealing of the skin. The body was sacred, her mother insisted, and need only be revealed to the Goddess and not another living soul. Perhaps her mother had learned that from her own mother?

Chanyn reached for another dress, but found it cut in the same way. In fact, all the dresses revealed some part of a woman's body. In the end, she assumed this was the way women dressed in the city.

Dain had found her family. He would arrive at her door shortly to escort her to their home. After three days here, it would be her first trek into the city proper.

Chanyn hadn't been out of the house since she'd come to stay with Dain and Khial. She hadn't minded. She spent the second day walking the gardens of the estate, and that night meandering the rooms. Dain had joined her and given her another tour with tales of his mother and fathers. Chanyn could tell that he had come from a loving home.

She and Dain had been alone and talking together for hours that day, the day after his proposal. She'd expected him to embrace her, to kiss her, to hold her hand.

He did none of those.

He would lightly touch her elbow to guide her in the direction he wanted her to go next. Always smiling at her, with that bit of awe at the corners of his eyes, he'd lean in every once in a while, and mock whisper something mundanely scandalous that he and Khial had done when they were younger. He'd smile or laugh with delight at her observations.

Dain was so easy to be with. Chanyn could easily picture them old and gray, walking and talking in this same companionable way. An ease, a sense of peace, settled over her.

The next day started the same way. A walk in the gardens. A chance meeting with Dain in a different part of the house. Another sociable talk, more delighted smiles, followed by companionable silences as they simply sat and gazed out over Dain's land.

Yes, Chanyn was sure she could get used to this.

A knock sounded at Chanyn's door. She recovered from her startle and went to answer it.

Dain stood on the other side, dressed impeccably in a white shirt, tan slacks, and his ever-present smile. But this smile was different. This smile didn't quite meet his eyes and that was because they swept over her body instead of looking into her eyes.

"How are you this morning, m'lady?"

Chanyn had a brief instinct to cover herself. But this was Dain. He'd never leered at her. In fact, she wasn't sure she'd mind if he did.

When she didn't respond immediately, Dain finally looked up and into her eyes, concern itched in the corners. It dawned on her where this concern came from.

"He didn't hurt me," Chanyn said. Dain must have been looking for evidence of foul play at the hands of the Pleasure Hound, Jian. "It was entirely my fault that..."

Here Chanyn paused. She felt mortified to explain further any of what she and Jian had been doing. Which was absurd, since she'd seen Dain doing the same thing with Khial. And she'd likely be doing the same thing with both of them soon.

Chanyn looked away, face heating.

"I believe it was entirely your fault," Dain said.

Chanyn's mortification couldn't have increased more. So she'd broken yet another social custom. What did this mean? Would Dain no longer want a wild, untrainable thing such as her? Would he send her away?

But then he laughed.

Chanyn looked up. His green eyes were filled once more with amusement. He shook his head as he gazed at her.

"You almost scared the poor man off. We're lucky he's agreed to return." Dain continued laughing, but when his eyes connected with Chanyn's he sobered. He reached out for her hand and enfolded it in the crook of his elbow. "There's much you need to learn, Chanyn."

Dain walked them down the hall, down the stairs, and out the door. "You're used to being someone's servant, out of necessity. Women here are objects of worship. *They* are served. You upset the balance when you seek to serve a man. You must let the hound do his work and serve you."

"I will," Chanyn said. "I promise."

Dain smiled at her, friendly once again. They stopped in the driveway. He took her hand from the crook of his elbow and brought it to his lips.

Chanyn's eyes watched the movement. Her mouth parted as Dain's lips met her skin. They felt soft and warm. She sighed, wishing those lips had met another target.

Dain's intelligent eyes swept over her face like he was reading a book. He straightened. Placing his hands on her shoulders, he leaned in. The brush of his lips against hers was soft. Softer than Chanyn had expected. She felt both his top and bottom lip. But they were dry now and a bit chilled. His nose squished her own. She could feel beads of sweat on his forehead. And the flutter of his eyelashes as they opened.

In the books, the women always felt a shift take place in their minds, a skipped beat of their heart. Chanyn felt... normal. She must be doing something wrong. She wondered if she should open her eyes, too. And so she did.

They stared at each other, lips still pressed together. They stayed that way for a moment; neither pulling away, nor pressing things any further. Then Dain's eyes flicked to the left. He jerked back from her, holding her at arms distance. Chanyn turned to look over her shoulder.

Khial stood staring at the two of them. His eyes wide in shock. His normally scowling mouth agape in disbelief.

Dain cleared his throat, his thumb brushing over his mouth. "We're going into the city." He had to clear his throat again as the words garbled. "If you would like to join us?"

Khial stared at Dain another moment. His eyes narrowed as though the English language were foreign to him. Finally, he blinked and walked into the house without a word.

Dain hesitated, one foot turned toward the house, one hand still on Chanyn's shoulder. In the end, he sighed and turned to her. The smile that stretched across his face aimed for easy, but it looked weary.

"Ready to go."

It wasn't a question as he handed her into the car and they took off.

They were silent for a while.

"You know that I like you, Chanyn." Dain turned to glance at her from the driver's panel. "I like you very much."

There was such earnestness in his eyes. Earnestness that Chanyn didn't need to see. She knew he spoke the truth.

"I like you very much too, Dain."

He nodded as though he wasn't quite sure and had to roll the words around in his head a bit. "Khial... Khial didn't grow up in a loving family. He has a rough time with new people. But he is the most loyal, passionate, loving human being I know."

Dain paused, his fingers gripping the steering wheel. Chanyn could see the blood draining as he clenched harder.

"Please," his voice strained with the plea. "You just need to give him some time."

Desperation replaced Dain's earnestness. It was Dain who proposed—Khial made no such overtures. But the two males were a packaged deal, a package Chanyn wanted to be bound to; to be bundled in the love she saw that Dain and Khial shared. She would do whatever was necessary to get to that place.

"I will," Chanyn promised.

Dain nodded. Some of the blood returned to his fingers, but he continued to grip the steering wheel.

They pulled up before a mansion that rivaled Dain's place. It was a sprawling compound, all on one floor. The gardens were lush with color. In the distance, Chanyn could see men, young and mature, in the fields picking the produce of the fertile earth. The fertile lands went on as far as she could see. The shock must have shown on her face.

"You come from a very powerful family Chanyn. The women inside that compound are leaders in the government and sciences."

Chanyn felt a pang. She didn't excel at either of those. Her mother had always been disappointed that her daughter had no head for the large volumes of reading necessary to master the political or technical sciences. Chanyn was always far more interested in the social constructs she found in fiction.

Dain was at her door handing her out. He walked to the gates with her, her hand once more tucked into the crook of his arm. "I'll wait for you right here."

Chanyn's head whipped to his. "You're not coming in?"

Dain laughed shaking his head. "I don't think your family would be interested in my company."

"But you're to be my husband. Shouldn't my family get to know you better?"

Dain gazed down at her, wonder and awe alight on his face alongside something else Chanyn couldn't name. He moved a hair from her brow. Chanyn had always read of men doing that to women. She found it pleasant.

"This world no longer works that way, Chanyn. Since the Great Destruction, men's opinions are seldom tolerated, much less asked for. You may have come into this world with only the clothes on your back and a stack of books, but you came with far more power and influence than I or my wealth could ever afford me."

The door opened then. An older man with an expressionless face stood stiffly on the other side. His gaze flicked up in surprise at Dain's hand on Chanyn's cheek.

Dain put his hand away. "Lady Chanyn to see the ladies of the house."

The servant nodded and Chanyn was handed inside. Dain did not cross the threshold. He gave her an encouraging smile before the door was summarily shut in his face.

"This way, if you please." The servant led Chanyn through an ornate walkway. Pictures of great women lined the walls. Many Chanyn did not recognize, though some she did from the pictures in books. There were queens of the lands once called Egypt and Europe. Goddesses of the land of Greece. There were also great warriors depicted. Female leaders from the twentieth who had done battle with men before the destruction. Warriors such as Hillary Clinton and Sasha Obama.

And then she saw them, the powerful women of today. There were four of them, gathered in a small sitting room sipping tea..

One was an elderly woman. She reminded Chanyn of Jian with her olive toned skin and lifted eyes.

To one side of her sat a mature woman. She was as dark as the earth. She held a reader in her hands instead of a teacup. She tapped quickly, her eyes scanning fast.

Off to the side, on a settee, sat two young ladies. One swirled her tea and gazed out the window. The other tapped her teacup impatiently as she gazed at the clock.

"Lady Chanyn," announced the male servant, bowing deeply before retreating from the room. Chanyn watched his retreat and then turned back. All eyes were on her. Assessing. No one jumped up and ran to her with arms out-flung. No one smiled a warm welcome. No one even spoke.

"Hello," Chanyn tried.

"Come in, child," said the elder woman. "We do not hover in doorways like manservants."

Chanyn made her way over. Unsure where to sit, she decided to wait for an invitation. When none came, Chanyn decided to try talking again.

"My name is Chanyn. My mother was—"

"We know who you are. And I should know my own daughter's name."

So, the elderly lady was her grandmother. Her pinched face was quite like Chanyn's mother's.

"The least Cylia could have done was to raise the child with some form of manners. Sit, child."

Chanyn chose an empty chair nearer the younger ladies. She lowered herself, and decided to keep her mouth shut. Again, there was silence as they all openly eyed Chanyn.

"Would you like some tea, cousin?" This came from one of the younger girls on the settee. The one with flaming red hair and golden-brown eyes like Chanyn's. Only the brown of the girl's eyes was solid and the gold lay at the edges.

Cousin, she'd said. Chanyn smiled at the girl and nodded.

"I'm Alyss," she said with a smile, handing over a full cup. This is my sister Merlyn."

Merlyn nodded and then her dark head went back to staring down the clock. "Mama, I've met her. Now may I return to the labs?"

"No," said her mother, which would make her Chanyn's aunt. "Custom dictates that we spend at least one quarter of an hour with a guest. Two when it's family."

With that said, they all sat in silence for another five minutes. Alyss stirred her tea. Merlyn watched the clock. Chanyn's grandmother continued to stare at her. Her aunt continued to tap at her device.

Finally Chanyn couldn't take the silence any longer. "My mother passed away," she said. All eyes fell upon her. "Nearly six months ago, now."

She allowed the weight of her statement to settle and take root in the members of her family. Again, no one said anything for a moment. Until finally her grandmother sighed.

"Well, did she at least postulate a new unified theory of relativity?"

Chanyn wasn't sure what that meant. Her ignorance must have shown on her face.

"Your mother was trying to develop an all-encompassing explanation of the physical aspects of the universe," her grandmother said with great irritation.

Oh, Chanyn thought. So that's what her mother had been doing with all those books and experiments. Chanyn could never quite grasp the lengthy explanations her mother tried to stuff into her head.

"Cylia felt she couldn't focus with all the worldly things around her, especially *men*." Her grandmother spat the word men.

"I don't know if she... postulated one," Chanyn shrugged. "She didn't tell me."

Her aunt frowned in disappoint and then went back to her device. Chanyn felt the disappointment was directed at her ignorance instead of her mother's failure. The two women were definitely sisters. Chanyn remembered that frown all too well.

Chanyn looked around the room. There were no pictures on the walls depicting family portraits. "I wondered," Chanyn began and then cleared her throat as her grandmother stared at her. "I wondered about my fathers?"

"What about them?"

"I'd like to meet them," she said to her grandmother.

Now all of the women in the room regarded her curiously.

"We have their files..." her grandmother looked around the room, "...somewhere. Your mother sent them away once she confirmed your gender."

Chanyn could only blink. She'd always assumed that when her mother left, her fathers remained behind hoping that one day their daughter would find them again.

"I hear you were found by Lord Dain and Lord Khial," Alyss said beside her. She laid a tentative hand on Chanyn's wrist. "Did they take liberties with you out in the wild?" Alyss jerked her hand back as though she might catch a contagion.

"No," Chanyn said. "Dain and Khial have been nothing but good to me." Well, Dain anyway. "They are gentlemen."

Her aunt looked up from her tablet and laughed at this. "Gentlemen?" she said. "The son of a sex actress and the son of a murderess."

Chanyn had known about Dain's parents' employment, but this new revelation about Khial's parents made her heart thud. Is that why Dain had white-knuckled the steering wheel? Because he knew they'd tell her about Khial's background?

"Now, Lady Danyell didn't kill her mates herself," her grandmother corrected. "She simply drove the men to kill one another. It was a fascinating experiment if you ask me."

"I was quite surprised the Sisterhood had her locked away. It was only two men after all."

"Men are people, too, Mother." This from the clock-watching Merlyn.

"I didn't realize you were raising a sympathist, Angyla," their grandmother admonished.

Merlyn's brown skin appeared to flush a shade darker and she took up her sentry with the clock once more.

"She's young. All childrearing theories say they are supposed to rebel around this age," Angyla dismissed her daughter, and continued with her previous line of conversation. "I had no respect for the psychological arts before Lady Danyell's scandal. After the incident, I actually downloaded one of her books. But I found her work tedious poppycock and quickly discarded it."

"Whatever is the matter with the child?" Chanyn's grandmother stared at her with a hand over her chest.

"I think she may be in shock, grandmother." Alyss came around to the front of Chanyn. "She just learned she's been in the company of two unfit men."

Alyss patted her hand. Her touch was soothing, though Alyss assumed she soothed Chanyn's relief that she'd escaped from danger when in fact Chanyn was beside herself at the callousness of these women.

"Now, you will stay with us," Alyss said still stroking Chanyn's hand as though she were a frightened pet. "And we'll help you find suitable men to use for conception. Merlyn has contracted one male, and is still vetting potential seconds. I won't be of age for another year but I've declined to mate. I find the whole business distasteful."

Chanyn looked at the girl. She thought they were nearly the same in years, but Chanyn didn't have much experience to judge.

"If you don't have a mind for science, then you can become the family breeder." Alyss' eyes were alight, prideful that she'd solved this problem before any of the adult women could come to it.

"That's quite a good idea, Alyss," said their grandmother, appraising Chanyn anew. "It is high time we birthed more females into the family."

They all appraised Chanyn anew.

All her life Chanyn heard her mother's tales of leering men. But the way these women now eyed her, Chanyn felt leered at by the women.

She got up from her seat, turned, and without a word walked through the entryway, and out the door. Dain sat in the car with his head stretched back against the seat so that his neck was hyper-extended, his eyes closed. He jumped and clutched his heart when Chanyn opened the passenger side door.

"Take me home," she said.

Dain glanced at her, but asked no questions. A sad, sorry smile played at his lips. Chanyn wondered if he'd been worried about losing her to her family; or had he been worried Chanyn would cross that threshold and have her dreams of having a family dashed.

Dain turned the ignition and drove away from Chanyn's relatives and back to her new family.

CHAPTER TEN

FOR THE THIRD TIME, JIAN woke to the guttural sound of his own voice. It had happened twice before during the night. Visions of Chanyn's head bobbing up and down on his shaft. The feel of her lips like velvet on his skin. His shaft throbbed, his body thrashed, and his release, as he lay without the ring's obstruction, shook him awake.

This time he woke in the common room. A few eyes of the elderly monks slid his way in admonishment at disturbing their peaceful afternoon of silent reading and meditation. Jian shifted in his robes, an uncomfortable maneuver as he tried to cover the damp impression left by the still raging stiffness of his shaft.

"How's the training going, young pup?"

Even though Jian was well past his adolescence, he remained the youngest hound in the temple. With no clientele in the past few years, the newer recruits all left. Even Jian's fellow training mates had long since left. Those three males had been the last class of trainees at the temple. The young males had been inseparable in their youth and throughout training. Closer to Jian than his own flesh and blood; but as the temple waned and could no longer support them, they each left. Jian never considered leaving. Though, in the first few years after the scandal, he'd been afraid he'd be tossed out on his ear.

Elder Gerry had been the one to sponsor Jian into the temple. Over the years he'd become very much a father figure. He'd come to Jian's defense after the scandal, a move Jian was sure had cost him upward mobility within the temple ranks.

Elder Gerry looked at him now in his peaceful, untethered way. A look Jian tried to master.

"I do not anticipate it will take very long," Jian said, in answer to Elder Gerry's question about Chanyn's training.

Jian could already tell that Chanyn was orgasmic. Even in centuries past, both women and men considered the female orgasm to be elusive. It wasn't elusive. It simply required patience on the part of both parties.

A woman needed to be relaxed and trust her partner.

A man needed to have a working knowledge of a woman's anatomy and an attention span longer than a gnat's.

Lady Chanyn had relaxed almost instantly with him, and her trust came closely on its heels. In the past, with other women, it took Jian many sessions just to get to the point where they would arch into his touch. Chanyn was a responsive woman. Jian doubted he could take much of the credit for her pleasure.

"The first payment should be in our accounts," Jian said.

Elder Gerry nodded. "It is indeed. I've sent for supplies. With the next installment we will be able to repair the roof."

Elder Gerry put a gnarled hand on Jian's shoulder and gave him a squeeze. Most often, the monk wore a serene, expressionless mask upon his face. But just now, the old man's lips quirked up, his eyes alight with pride at his young protégé.

"Good work, Jian."

"I just hope that the brothers see it that way," Jian said. He looked around at the faces of the monks.

Elder Gerry's eyes followed Jian's. "Do you remember the first time we met?"

Jian did. He'd been living on the street.

"I was doing a walking meditation," Elder Gerry said. "You were out in a park when I saw you. You had come across a dog."

Jian remembered. It was a handsome looking dog, golden brown fur and pale eyes. His elder brother had a cocker spaniel. That small dog had taken to Jian and, for its love of another, his brother had abused it.

"I saw you reach out for the animal, intending to pet it," said Elder Gerry. "But it growled at you and bared its teeth."

"It bit me, actually."

The dog had been collared and was an unlikely case for rabies. If the animal had been rabid Jian would've likely died. A discarded street kid didn't have much access to a physic's medicinals.

"That it did," agreed Elder Gerry. "I watched the cloud of anger descend upon your face. I thought certainly you would strike out at the animal. But you didn't."

Jian had been angry at the animal. He'd intended an act of kindness and was stricken instead. Jian had always been slow to anger and slow to strike out. The bite was only a scratch. His feelings hurt more than his skin. A closer look at the animal showed that its leg was trapped under a fallen log.

"You paused and in an instant your face changed from anger to compassion. That's when I knew you were meant for this order. You saw that suffering comes from suffering. One doesn't cause injury unless they are hurt."

"The dog changed his attitude when I removed the log," Jian said.

"I remember it differently. The dog never ceased growling and snapping at you while you moved the log. It never changed. You did."

Elder Gerry must've seen the confusion that rested on Jian's face because he continued to clarify his lesson.

"You are still carrying the wounds of the incident from years ago."

Jian knew Elder Gerry no longer spoke of the wound from the dog's bite. He spoke of Jian's ill-fated love affair

"What would happen if you looked past the scar she left? Past the blame? Past the inward growling and snapping you do to yourself? What would you find?"

Elder Gerry didn't wait for Jian to answer. With one more squeeze and a nod, his open expression disappeared. It morphed once more into serenity, and the old man walked on.

Jian carried heavy feet over to a waterfall installation within the communal sanctuary. He reached a hand into the soft transparency of the fall, marveling that something so soft had the power to wear down vast lands. Much of the original continent of the north was under water, unable to withstand the power of water's insistence.

Jian folded his wet hand into his lap. He entwined his fingers, wet overlapping dry, and closed his eyes. Elder Gerry thought Jian should pause. And so he did. Tapping into the energy around him, Jian began to center his mind. He settled himself and peeled back the layers of that time five years ago.

In an instant, Jian felt drenched with sweat. The wound, though old, had never been treated. Beneath the surface, it festered. His heart became heavy. His hands began to shake. He could not go and do his duty to Lady Chanyn in such a condition. He would have to tend to this matter another time. He quickly packed the wound once more and focused on emptying his mind of all thought and feeling.

An hour later, he felt strong in body and spirit. Jian left the temple and headed towards his duty. But coming upon the home of Lord Dain brought to mind the memory of the last big house he'd been in before this one. He hadn't packed the old wound tightly enough, and it broke free and surfaced like a geyser.

Five years ago he'd come to a home like this one, prepared to offer for the woman he loved. Dressed in a regular man's clothes of slacks and a cotton shirt, Jian knocked on the door. When the door opened he was met by a number of men. They'd thrown him to the ground.

It had been raining earlier and he landed in the mud. His fine clothes ruined, but worse, when he glanced up he'd seen *her* in the second story window, watching. Her eyes looked at him as though she'd never known him. As though the sweet nothings she'd boldly whispered never passed her lips. With one final glance at Jian covered in the refuse of the street, she turned from the window and back to the luxuries within her home.

It was the second time Jian had been thrown out of a home. The first had been his mother's. Jian blinked back the memory, trying to stuff the old hurt down once more.

Though Lord Dain had invited him back, Jian took the steps warily. What would he feel if he looked past the blame? Jian knew the answer to that. He didn't need to unpack the wound from five years ago; there was a wound that preceded it. Beneath the second wound of rejection lay a foundation of hurt, of grief. The knowledge that he was not worthy of love. Not even from his own mother.

Jian took another moment to call to the Goddess for peace. And then he rang the doorbell.

A manservant answered the door to Lord Dain's home and Jian was admitted without ceremony. He found his own way to Lady Chanyn's room. He raised his hand to knock, but before his knuckles met wood, the door was thrown open.

Lady Chanyn stood on the other side. Eyes wide, a bit breathless, completely lovely.

"Lady Chanyn." Jian lowered his gaze and bowed.

When he rose she was frowning at him. She gave a barely perceptible nod of what seemed like acceptance and then stepped aside to allow him in.

The door closed them in and Jian had a moment of panic. She was barely covered. Her scent caught his nose and he swallowed. Big mistake. Her sweet taste now rolled on his tongue and down his throat.

Jian made a sound to clear his throat. Before he could speak, Lady Chanyn beat him to it.

"I'm really sorry, Jian. I see now that I have so much to learn."

As she spoke, Jian noticed something different about her. There was a determined set to her jaw, a steely resolve in the way she held her shoulders. The eyes that had been so innocent only a day before looked aged with some new knowledge.

"Please allow me to take the full weight of the blame," he said. "As your instructor, I should have informed you of the rules and expectations before beginning the lesson."

She smiled up at him, relieved. It was so easy to get lost in the pool of churning gold and bronze that were her eyes. Captivated by her gaze, Jian felt fullness settle in his body.

"I'll listen to you this time," she said. "I promise."

Jian nodded, still held in her gaze. A calming motion slowly crept up his arm. He realized it was his doing. Her hands were in his. He didn't remember reaching for them. His thumb traced a circular pattern in her palm. It was an erogenous zone. The zone connected directly to a woman's core.

Jian also noticed they stood thigh to thigh. Though he didn't remember stepping into her. With one of his thighs placed between hers, he could feel the heat emanating from her.

"I have something for you." Chanyn withdrew a package from the side table and handed it to him. Jian began to protest as she placed the package in his hands. It was improper for hounds to receive gifts directly. They were a communal lot and shared all earnings.

Jian prepared to hand the package back to her, but the shape and feel of it caught his curiosity. "What is this?"

Chanyn frowned. "I keep forgetting that these are no longer a part of your world."

Thoroughly curious now, Jian unwrapped the package and saw a firm piece of square leather that bound sheaths of thin material. He opened it and saw writing. He glanced up at Chanyn. "Is this a book?"

Chanyn nodded. "I brought it with me from my home. It's one of the only works of nonfiction that I actually enjoyed."

Jian turned the book's cover back over. *A Natural History of the Senses* by Diana Ackerman, it read. There was something about running his palm over the leather cover. Pinching the thin pages with his fingers. It was sensual for his mind.

He glanced up at Chanyn. She grinned proudly, watching him. He set the book down behind her, careful of the new treasure. Then he turned back to her.

"Take your clothes off, Chanyn."

She smiled at the mention of her name. Her free hand went to the tie at her collarbone. "Aren't we going to pray? I really liked the prayer." She gave the string a pull.

Jian sank to his knees along with the fabric and began to recite the prayer.

When he ended the prayer with "Ashe," he inhaled the scent emanating from Chanyn's core. They were not touching but he sensed the tremor that passed through her body.

He opened his eyes. She stood above him. He was on his knees ready to serve. This was the way of things. This is where Jian excelled.

"Go to the bed, Chanyn"

She went, on unsteady legs. Jian watched the up and down motion of her plump behind. Like her stomach in front, the flesh at her rear rose and fell like waves. She was not slightly built, like the women of the city. Her curves were an art in and of themselves. He could trace them with his eyes for hours before giving his fingers their turn.

When she reached the bed, she turned, awaiting further instruction.

Jian, still on his knees, folded his hands in his lap in simulation of the meditative pose that prepared him for this session. "Sit down," he instructed.

She did.

"Open your legs."

Chanyn hesitated. His eyes locked on hers, and waited.

Finally, she made up her mind and slowly spread her thighs. Jian didn't look. He kept his eyes on hers while he crawled on his knees to her.

She made no sound, but he knew her breaths had sped to pants because her chest rose and fell rapidly.

His eyes still glued to hers, he said, "For today's lesson, we're going to test a theory. Did your mother teach you about theories?"

She nodded.

"I have a theory," Jian undid the sash of his robes, eyes still on hers. "I think you may be multi-orgasmic."

Chanyn's eyes flared at that.

"I'm going to test that theory now. I will test it using three tools. First, I'm going to use my mouth. Second, my hands. And then finally my shaft."

Jian freed the robes from his shoulders. Chanyn watched them fall, and then her eyes held at the area between his legs.

Jian grabbed her chin and brought her gaze back to his. "Here are the rules. You are not allowed to touch my shaft. Not with your hands and not with your mouth."

There was a slight frown that came to her lips and he saw the disappointment in her eyes. Jian had to take a breath so as not to throw her down on the bed, like a Neanderthal of the twentieth century.

Chanyn nodded her understanding and agreement. In truth, Jian felt a bit of disappointment that she didn't argue.

"This is sacred work, Chanyn. Are you ready to begin?"

For the first time, worry creased Chanyn's brow. Jian stifled the temptation to smooth her worries from her brow. Had he been too harsh in his instructions?

"Are you frightened, Chanyn?"

"No, I'm just... I do have one question?"

Jian nodded. She looked down, a bit uncomfortable. He did not let her chin go. He splayed his fingers along her cheekbone. Her skin was soft against his fingers. "You can ask me anything without fear of judgment."

Her eyes came back to his. "I've read... in my books... that the first time... hurts."

Hounds didn't have many vices outside of sweet berries. They lived simply and didn't want for much. They were taught not to boast. They were taught to tell the truth.

"It will not hurt."

Chanyn looked as though she didn't believe him.

A confident gleam lit his eyes. "I'm very well trained, Lady Chanyn. Anything that I do to you will bring pleasure, and only pleasure. This I promise you."

He held her gaze so that she felt the full weight of his vow.

She swallowed.

"Shall we begin?"

She nodded.

Jian continued to gaze into her eyes. He wanted to see the moment she gave over to his ministrations. Keeping one hand on her chin, the other sought her heat. He found her wet.

Chanyn gasped when Jian's thumb made contact with her clitoris.

Her eyes widened, then narrowed. "I thought you said you were going to start with your tongue."

Jian bit his lip to stop himself from bursting into laughter. "Do not contradict your teacher."

She grinned at him. Jian had his hands on the warm treasure of a woman for the first time in five years, but it was that unabashed smile that sent warmth spreading throughout his whole body. His heart pounded with want inside his chest.

Chanyn began to pant from his manipulations. He knew she would close her eyes and fall back onto the mattress soon. That she would give herself over to the feeling and get lost inside herself. But she didn't close her eyes. Her gaze stayed locked with his. She let him see everything.

He saw surprise, pleasure, ache, desperation. All of it she shared with him.

True to her word, she did not touch him. Her hands clutched the sheets. Her heels left the floor to balance on the balls of her feet. This motion tilted her hips to him. Jian's mouth watered with the desire to taste her.

Not yet. He wanted to see her fall apart first. He didn't have to wait long.

Her hips began to move involuntarily. Her eyes glazed, half closed. Still, she never broke from his gaze.

Now Jian wanted her eyes to stay open. He'd felt women's pleasure many times over, but he'd never seen it. He'd never looked into a woman's eyes as she orgasmed. He didn't realize he wanted that, until he'd nearly grasped it.

Chanyn was close. Any minute now she would close her eyes, give over to the pleasure, and Jian would be shut out.

Any minute now.

She was going to close them and shut him out... any minute now.

With a gasp Chanyn threw her head back.

"Oh, goddess," she shouted.

An instant later, her head came back up.

"Jian," she groaned his name, her eyes wide as her muscles began to convulse.

Chanyn grabbed onto his shoulders and held on. The move hit him like a meteoric impact. Jian's world shifted off its axis as shudders continued to rake Chanyn's body and still she did not take her eyes from his.

When she came back to herself, a small smile broke over her lips and a girlish giggle escaped her mouth. "That—" she began, but couldn't finish.

Jian lifted her up and tossed her back on the bed. Like a caveman, he was on her. Head buried between her thighs, mouth devouring her wet heat.

Chanyn arched off the bed, but Jian pinned her down with a hand to her chest. Instantly she began to tremble and gasp. She panted his name like a chant, intermixed with nonsensical cries of pleasure.

Jian was a man possessed as he swirled his tongue up and down her labia. Coming up for air, he did not relent on her pleasure. He slid one then a second finger inside her still quivering heat. He did not yet stroke. He stretched his body alongside hers. Legs entwined, bellies and chests touching. Jian gazed down at her face.

Chanyn was flushed. Her hands were thrown over her head. Her lips parted. Her chest heaving.

Responsive indeed.

When she realized she was being watched, she took her hands from her eyes. The orbs were pleasure glazed. Her mouth tried to work, but no sounds would come out. She raised a hand and slowly, tentatively placed it on his chest.

Her eyes asked, *Is this okay?*

With his free hand, Jian wiped the hair from her face, then went further and smoothed that line of worry from her brow. Deciding she'd had enough time to catch her breath, he began to stroke her core. Chanyn's eyes fluttered, but still they did not shut. They stared up at him in wonder.

The feeling of fullness was becoming overwhelming to Jian. His shaft ached to enter her. His very blood ached to join with hers. He could see the pounding of his own heart in his chest by the slight twitch of her fingers as they pet its cage.

Jian got down to work. His fingers worked a soft patch of nerves at the front of her pelvis. Within a matter of moments, Chanyn was jerking, convulsing. Still her eyes did not shut. She looked at him in complete shock as she trembled and groaned once more.

Jian could take it no more. He withdrew his fingers and placed himself between her legs. Chanyn welcomed his weight by spreading her thighs wider. Jian aligned himself at her entrance and put in the tip.

Chanyn sighed. Her warm breath tickling Jian's cheek.

He reached around her to grab her rear with both hands. Eyes still locked on hers, he entered her in one thrust.

This time her eyes did close. And she screamed.

The scream was not one of pain. The impact and angle of the

thrust wrenched another orgasm from her. He felt her clutching all around his shaft. If he hadn't been wearing the ring he would have spilled inside her.

He'd never before thought of implanting his seed in a woman. He couldn't have those thoughts now. He had a job to do. A job he was doing splendidly, at the moment. Again, much of the credit had to go to Chanyn. She was beyond his wildest predictions. That was her third orgasm. Never had he been with a woman so responsive.

She was just returning to consciousness. Her breathing slowing. Her fingers trembling on his chest. Her legs closed around his back letting him know she would take more.

She gazed at him. Her fingers snaked up behind his neck. She pulled him down. Ready to give her the closeness that women often needed after orgasm, Jian went willingly.

When something wet and warm met his lips, at first Jian wasn't sure what to think. It was the most pleasant sensation he'd ever felt. Just as pleasant as when Chanyn had put her lips on his—

Jian gasped. Chanyn was kissing him. He'd never been kissed by a woman before.

The gasp opened his mouth and she tentatively slipped her tongue in.

His shaft was buried in a woman and now his tongue. Jian knew he should pull away, but the sensation was the most pleasurable of his life. His body would not listen to his mind. Or perhaps his mind was on board. In either case, as Chanyn stroked him with her tongue, Jian began to stroke her with his shaft.

Jian never even dreamed of such a thing. Kissing a woman. Becoming a hound had been a lucky accident. Most men never touched a woman, much less joined with them. And kissing one? The intimate experience was only reserved for bonded triads, and not always. To be sure, men kissed each other in the act of sex. Jian had always enjoyed the practice with his male partners. But just as there was something different when Chanyn had taken his shaft into her mouth, there was again something different now that his mouth was joined with a woman's.

Jian felt as though it was a small piece of heaven.

He also felt that he was in serious trouble.

Jian brought Chanyn to climax twice more before she began to doze off. As her eyes were now closed, he stared at her for long moments, holding her in the cradle of his arms. It was an ancient prescription for the aftercare of sex. Most modern women didn't care for it. Instead, they were ready to go off and tend to the pressing matters of the world after their carnal lessons. Jian knew Chanyn would want it. In truth, he needed it himself. Though he hadn't climaxed once, his body felt the effects of their time together. So he held her tightly, and closed his eyes momentarily to all the thoughts and feelings that demanded to be worked out in that instant.

When next Jian opened his eyes, the sun was kissing his cheek. With dread, he realized he'd spent the night.

Entirely unprofessional.

He and Chanyn were wrapped around each other, a tangle of arms and limbs with her head nestled into his chest. There would be no way of not waking her up. He began extracting himself from her as gently as he could.

When her eyes opened, she smiled at him. Now out of bed, Jian turned away and reached for his robes. He heard the rustle of sheets as she sat up.

"I've done something wrong again, haven't I?"

Jian opened his mouth to deny it, but he wouldn't lie to her. He didn't want to cast dispersion on the gift of the kisses she'd given him.

So he told a different truth. "It was unprofessional of me to impose on you for the night, my lady."

She looked relieved. "Oh, I didn't mind."

Jian arranged his robes over his naked body. "In any case, I'll be taking my leave."

"But I'll see you again? Tonight?"

The eagerness in her eyes nearly did him in. "You truly do not need much training, Lady Chanyn. You are quite prepared for your bondmates."

Chanyn's face fell. She worried the sheets with her hands, a crease settled between her brows once more. Jian felt the urge to go and relieve her of the sheets. To kiss the worry from each finger. To smooth the crease of her forehead.

He stayed rooted where he was.

"I've been thinking," she began and then paused. Glancing at him, then away. "Dain is really nice. He's been so good to me. He arranged... this," she motioned between Jian and herself, "so that I would know what I was getting into before entering a triad with a bonded pair."

Chanyn straightened her shoulders, blanket clutched to her breasts, eyes square on his. "Dain said it was my choice who I wanted to mate with."

Jian's eyes widened as he came to understand the meaning behind her words. She was opening her mouth to speak again.

"And I just don't feel for him the way I—"

"Lady Chanyn, if I may." He bowed, stalling for time against the protesting beats of his heart. "You should not make any decisions directly after sex. Orgasms can cloud your judgment."

He chanced a look at her. He watched in slow motion as her shoulders slumped and her face fell.

"Oh," her voice was so small. "I see."

She avoided his eyes. After a night of gazing into them openly, Jian felt the weight of the loss.

"It has been my pleasure to serve you, Lady Chanyn." Jian bowed, and turned away from her. Sash in hand, he hesitated at the door. Wondering if there were manservants waiting on the other side to carry him bodily down the stairs and then toss him out the door.

But when he opened the door, he found the hall empty. He made his way down the stairs and was nearly to the front door when a voice called him.

"Brother Jian, Lord Dain would like to see you," said a manservant.

Jian took a moment to gather himself, and then turned and marched down the hall as though to his own execution. When he arrived at Lord Dain's office, he saw Lord Khial leaning against a window gazing out. Lord Dain stood very close to the man, nuzzling the side of his face. Lord Khial stubbornly ignored the affection and Lord Dain sighed. Lord Dain must have sensed Jian because he turned towards the door.

Jian steeled himself for an explosive confrontation.

He was met with a friendly smile.

Lord Dain motioned Jian to a chair before his desk. Jian moved tentatively into the room and took the proffered seat. Lord Dain sat in his high back chair and steepled his fingers. Lord Khial remained with his gaze fixed out the window.

"And how is our lady?"

Jian blinked. There was no accusation or disapproval in Lord Dain's tone. He seemed genuinely curious as though a Pleasure Hound sleeping over were the most natural thing in the world.

"She's... well," Jian said. Then seeing an out, he continued. "In fact, I wanted to talk with you about her progress."

Lord Dain nodded encouragingly for Jian to continue.

"She has exceeded my expectations."

Lord Dain smiled at this, as though a proud parent pleased by a child's progress.

"There's not much more I can teach her in the way of orgasm. I believe she is ready for the two of you."

At this, Lord Khial whipped his head around to Jian and glared. Jian blinked at the bitterness in the man's glare. He remembered Chanyn saying she didn't think the male liked her. A sudden protective instinct swept through Jian. But he reminded himself that Chanyn was not his responsibility. The temple and the hounds were.

Jian turned his attention to Lord Dain.

"I believe my work here is done," said Jian. He rose to leave.

Lord Dain's smile morphed into a frown. He inhaled deeply and then sighed.

"Brother Jian, would you please have a seat?" Lord Dain waited until Jian took his seat before speaking. "We're very pleased with your work with Lady Chanyn. But we still require your help."

Lord Dain spared a glance over his shoulder at his mate. Lord Khial refused to meet his eyes and glared out the window. Jian couldn't fathom what this was all about, but he was sure he wasn't going to like it. He simply wanted to leave this house and return to the sanctity of the temple. With the money he made, he might be able to turn things around. And so long as word of the ring mishap, and the overnight stay mishap, didn't get out, perhaps the temple might acquire another client or two.

The thought of training more women left a lump in Jian's stomach where only moments ago it had burned for Chanyn. Last night with Chanyn had been the most intense experience of his life. He knew that anything after would pale in comparison. The very thought of an *after* left him cold.

"I'm in need of an heir."

Jian whipped his head to Lord Dain.

"Lady Chanyn has accepted... our proposal. Neither Lord Khial, nor I, have ever been with a woman and we'd like you to forgo training and move directly to conception."

Jian couldn't help but notice that Lord Dain continued to use the word *we* though Lord Khial's posture screamed his distaste.

"We know that when conception is attempted under the hand of a Pleasure Hound," Lord Dain continued, "the success rate is always positive. And that the conception of female children is also at a high rate with the assistance of a hound. That is why we hired you. We need to conceive rather quickly, and we need your help."

Jian watched Lord Dain as he toyed with the collar of his shirt. The thought of those blunt fingers on Chanyn's skin made Jian's head hurt. The idea of watching another male take his—

Jian stopped the thought before it could complete itself. "I have responsibilities at the temple—"

"I am prepared to make it worth your while," Lord Dain interrupted him. "I know that your temple is in some financial straits. If Lady Chanyn conceives in the next month, the temple never has to worry about its finances, ever again. I promise you that."

Lord Dain released his collar and reached out his hand to Jian.

"Do we have a deal?"

PART TWO

CHAPTER ONE

SO THIS IS LOVE.

It was nothing like in the books. Chanyn couldn't focus. Food had no taste. There was a physical ache in her heart. She knew it was too soon to call it love, but he'd touched her deeply, and then walked away.

So this is heartbreak.

It was nothing like in the books. Chanyn couldn't focus. Food had no taste. There was a physical ache in her heart. She knew it was too soon to call it over. He still might come back.

Chanyn trudged through the paths of the gardens. Dain's mother returned to the Goddess many years ago, and still her flower garden thrived. Dain believed his mother's love was so deep it had yet to run out of her garden.

Chanyn did not discount Dain's belief. Flowers and plants that had no business growing in the southwestern part of the continent thrived in the soil. Thanks to her time in the reference section of her former home, she could identify many of the plants before her. She picked out the rare Desert Lily straight away. The plant's tall green shaft reached her breastbone. Its blooming, white petals hung low.

Chanyn turned away. She shook her head, trying to clear the carnal images the innocent plant brought to her mind. Farther down the path, Ocotillos stood tall and plentiful. Chanyn stretched a hand towards the red buds. They were hot and throbbing, ready to burst into bloom at any minute.

She pulled her hands back and covered her heated face.

That night, the last night they spent together, she'd thought Jian felt what she did. The way he held and caressed her. The way he looked into her soul. The way he kissed her until she couldn't tell where she ended and he began. Jian had pressed her body into his as though he would join them together permanently.

But the next morning he'd separated himself so easily, left so fast. He'd said holding her through the night had been a mistake, unprofessional. Had she just been a job to him?

An ornate white bench sat a few paces away, surrounded by a flowering bush. Chanyn settled down on it and surveyed the bush. She ran her fingers down the petals of a flower that looked like a rose, but not quite. The stem had a thick, sturdy hide. The fragrance was musky, not sweet. The deep blue petals, which were shaped like the chambers of a heart, looked soft, but felt rough. As her fingers caressed the petals, the bloom slowly closed itself off, shrinking away from her touch. Chanyn's index finger caught on one of the sharp thorns.

"Ouch!" Chanyn yanked her hand away from the fickle bouquet. She placed her hands in her lap and sighed.

From a distance, she heard the gravel of a conveyance approaching. Her heart kicked into gear. She bounced up onto her toes and took off towards the edge of the property. The soles of her shoes were flat. She'd given up on heels the second day of her stay.

Chanyn reached the edge of the property before the car stopped.

Her body ground to a halt, her stomach clenched, the disappointment a heavy weight. It was only a deliveryman.

Chanyn chastised herself. Monks were humble beings. They didn't own extravagant things like conveyances. If Jian were coming, he would walk.

The deliveryman left his package and was off. Chanyn watched him go down the street. She knew where the Temple of the Pleasure Hounds stood. She'd walked by the property for the past two days. Dain had had an appointment that kept him away for a full day. As he left, she'd noticed wariness in the corner of his eyes. Before she could ask him what the matter was, Khial herded him out the door. Chanyn assumed the pressure behind Dain's eyes was disappointment in her behavior with Jian, and driving her tutor away with her silly overtures of love; aborted before she could even lay her feelings on the table.

Tired of her life of leisure after only a week, Chanyn asked to accompany Rianald as he ran his errands. She'd wanted to see the city, she told him. And she had wanted to explore this new land she now lived in. It was not what Chanyn expected.

The part of the city where they lived was clean and safe. The building faces all freshly painted. Round domes sheathed the tops of all buildings, the tips pointing toward the Goddess. The grass below grew green and level. Women strolled the streets in finery. Some were on the arms of men but mostly the men trailed behind. Unattached men looked Chanyn over with interest, glancing first at her ringless hand, then her breasts. The women gave Chanyn curt, suspicious glances. Many spoke rudely behind their hands. Chanyn heard the words "wild" whispered more than once. Not one female came up and asked Chanyn where she got her dress, or paid her a compliment on her shoes, like they did in the books. When one female's flowered cap caught Chanyn's eye, Chanyn approached. Only to have the girl grow wide-eyed and retreat behind her males. Chanyn didn't approach another soul.

With Dain away, and Khial forever attached to his hip, and Jian missing in action, for the past two days Chanyn had been alone. It was worse than five months alone in the ruins without her mother. People surrounded her, but the distance of the crowd crushed her spirit.

Chanyn wrapped her arms around herself at the memory. Then her ears perked up. A sweet sound lured her back to the house. She knew it was Khial playing his instrument. He and Dain were back. Chanyn made her way through the home, up to the second floor. The music lured her past her bedroom.

She'd never been this far into the recesses of the house.

Rianald came out of a door. When he saw her he smiled, but the smile didn't reach his eyes. He looked down at the door, hesitated for a brief second, and then left it ajar. He passed Chanyn with a slight bow and continued on down the steps.

Chanyn looked at the door, hesitating. This was obviously both Dain and Khial's bedroom, a bedroom she no longer yearned to share.

Dain and Khial were in love. And so was she.

Dain told her she had a choice in whom she would mate. He'd promised she would not be forced. Chanyn knew Dain wanted to protect her, but she also knew he didn't love her. Dain loved Khial and he was being kind to her, like a friend. That was all there was between them. Friendship. And Chanyn was glad for that friendship, but she knew a marriage couldn't be founded upon it. Especially when there were more than two people in the relationship.

She decided to go in and tell Dain that. When she pushed the door open a bit further, she froze.

Deep brown furniture with black accents lay on the outskirts of the inherently masculine bedroom. A large sleigh bed dominated the area. Dain lay in bed, his eyes closed. Chanyn opened the door farther, and went in. Even from far away she could see that he was ill. His cheeks looked gaunt, sweat dampened his forehead.

As though sensing her, Dain opened his eyes and looked straight at her.

Chanyn saw the same joy he always displayed at seeing her. Dain was a truly loving person, and though she didn't love him in an intimate way, she did love him.

Chanyn read stories of small fish swimming under the bellies of great whales for protection. When Chanyn looked at Dain she felt her heart grow to the size of a whale. Her heart hurt to think that anything could be wrong with her friend.

Khial stopped playing and turned to see what caught Dain's attention.

"Good morning, my lady." Dain pushed himself up to sitting.

Chanyn came to the opposite side of the bed from Khial and sat upon the mattress. Taking Dain's hand in her own, she said, "You don't look well."

Dain's handsome face folded into a mock frown. "I just woke up. Let's see you first thing in the morning with bed head."

Chanyn felt Khial tense. She looked up and for once, Khial didn't scowl at her. But that was only because he looked too weary to manage the expression.

"What's wrong, Dain?" Chanyn asked.

Dain straightened himself with Khial's help. His face paled with the effort. His golden hair lacked its usual luster.

Chanyn hated it. She wanted to push him back down. She wanted to fold him in the covers to keep him warm. To swim above him, keeping him under the protection of her belly.

"I'm ill, Chanyn."

"I can see that," she said. "Can't we go to a physic?"

"We've been," Dain said. "Just yesterday. There's nothing that can be done. I'm going to die, Chanyn."

Chanyn's heart missed a beat. Her mouth lost its sense of taste, her body ached. Falling in love, having your heart broken, and hearing that you would soon lose a friend all felt exactly the same.

"It's my heart," Dain continued. "I was born with weak muscles. They didn't expect me to live past a year. But my parents told the doctors if my heart ailed me then I only need to be showered with love. And that's what they did. They took me home and celebrated each day of my life. I've lived far longer than I was meant to. I've had a wonderful, full life. I've known love."

Dain looked over at Khial. The other man grit his teeth and gripped his instrument, but it was the look of vulnerability on Khial's scowling face that broke Chanyn's heart once more.

Dain turned back to her. "I've been given far more than I could have ever asked for. And then, when I thought things could not have gotten any better for me, I met you."

Chanyn gasped. "Me?"

Dain grinned. "I thought you were an angel when you saved us from that boar. I was right." Dain squeezed her hand. "There's not much I can make right in this world, being a man. But I can leave the people I care about in the comfort that was given to me."

"I don't understand what you mean, Dain."

"Khial's family wealth was claimed by the Sisterhood for his mother's crimes. My wealth cannot pass to Khial being that he's a man. When we are bonded, all of my wealth will pass to you, and both you and Khial will be cared for."

Chanyn looked to Khial for clarification, but he would not meet her eyes. She'd come into this room to break the engagement with

Dain. The worst she expected when she crossed the threshold was losing a friend, losing a home. She'd never fathomed that her friend's life would be put in her hands. But as she was about to learn, it didn't end there.

"My uncle will contest the transfer of wealth when I'm gone. To ensure that he cannot, I'll need to leave an heir. A male heir would make things difficult, but not impossible for my uncle to win a case in a court of law. A female heir will leave no room for argument."

Chanyn trembled. Not in the way when Jian touched her. Not in the way when her mother raised her voice.

Dain reached for her other hand. "I'm sorry that I won't be here to walk the gardens with you, or teach you those board games." He tried for a smile but failed. "I know I should have told you from the beginning. It was wrong of me to mislead you. But I couldn't stand the thought of you alone in those ruins. And I didn't want you in a union with males who didn't care about you. I hope this doesn't change your mind?"

How could she do this? Have a child with another man? A dying man. Her dying friend whom she loved, but in a non-intimate way. Her friend who'd withheld information, but only because he thought he could give her the life he felt she deserved. Neither her heart nor her mind knew which way to turn.

"The monk, Brother Jian, has agreed to help."

Chanyn's mind went blank and her weary heart hit the floor.

"He has a few conditions, though," Dain continued.

So, Jian had agreed to this scheme with a head level enough to make stipulations. Chanyn's mind fogged. Ice ran through the chambers of her heart.

"He insists that we formalize the bond before we begin any conception rituals."

Meaning Jian wanted Chanyn to understand that he was beyond her reach before he touched her again. So, she had her answer on whether or not he felt anything for her.

CHAPTER TWO

KHIAL WATCHED CHANYN TAKE THE news. The blood drained from her brown face. The light wept out of her eyes.

For days, he'd been concerned that she desired Dain's heart. It was clear that she cared for Dain. Care and desire were two different animals.

He'd watched Chanyn mope around the garden the past two mornings. The sadness of her solitary walks was not the same as the sadness of her silent vigil as she watched Dain fall asleep. Chanyn cared for Dain, but her heart belonged to another.

The thought should have eased Khial entirely. It didn't. Neither of them would be allowed to keep the men they desired. This world was cruel. In the face of the Goddesses' cruelty, Khial did what he always did. He picked up his bow and played.

Music had been Khial's outlet, likely from the time he was in the womb. His mother published a study on the effects of different genres of music on a growing fetus. Khial read the paper once he reached school age. Apparently, that study was his first failure at meeting his mother's expectations. In the study, his mother postulated that playing classical music would breed females. To her ire, Khial came into the world with one too many appendages, along with an affinity for classical music.

When Khial was older, his mother tested the theory of whether spanking a child had a better outcome than issuing time outs. Spanking a female child was outlawed. But no such law existed when it came to a difficult to handle, hard-headed, male child. The problem Khial's mother came across? Khial never misbehaved. Left alone, Khial stayed quietly in his room from sunup to sundown, practicing his instrument. His mother focused on that. If Khial made a mistake, he would be alternately beaten by one of his fathers or have his instrument taken away as a time out.

Khial's response? He stopped practicing at home. He feigned giving up the violin altogether, and in time, his mother forgot that experiment and moved on to worse. Khial did not give up music. It had settled in his very soul. He practiced at school instead.

One day, while practicing a particularly difficult piece, Dain materialized from the shadows. Khial shrank away, horrified that someone heard his repeated mistakes. He flinched when Dain came closer, expecting to be hit or ridiculed. Dain came up to him, glowing smile in place, and called Khial's music beautiful. Khial had never received praise for his playing. From that day forward his soul belonged to Dain. He played for Dain every day after.

Khial played that song now, that difficult piece from their first meeting. He found it as complex now as he had as a child. The pads of his fingers bruised as he vibrated the strings to affect the mourning sounds the notes demanded. His bow glided up and down on the low string as he approached the ending. Like always, his fingers tired, his arms ached, and he tripped on the last note. And like always, he flinched from the expectation of one of his fathers' strike.

"That was beautiful."

Khial startled. Chanyn's liquid eyes regarded him, her mouth parted. He saw unmasked joy on her face.

He stared for a second, committing it to memory before admitting, "I messed up."

Chanyn shrugged her slim shoulders. "I couldn't tell."

Khial watched her supple breasts rise and fall beneath the cotton. Her nipples were erect. They weren't when he'd begun playing; he'd noticed, before closing his eyes and shutting her out. But now he saw the tips poking brazenly through the cloth, right at him. Had his music done that?

Khial turned from her. He set the violin against the side table. Then he turned back to his lover and pulled the blanket over Dain, who slept peacefully. Chanyn pulled up the end on her side of their bed. She brushed a curl out of Dain's eye. Dain sighed but didn't wake.

"You love him, don't you?"

Conflict etched on her face as she looked between himself and Dain.

"The monk," Khial clarified.

She took a steadying breath and then met Khial's eyes. He thought she'd deny it. Now that Dain offered her a fortune, a fortune she need do little to earn. Sleeping with Dain was a joy, Khial would know. He'd done the research and written the definitive study on the subject. She need only lay on her back, enjoy the ride, and then soon there would be no ties. When Dain... left, Khial certainly wouldn't be sticking around as her mate. So, yes. Khial expected she would definitely deny her love for the hound.

Once more, the Lady Chanyn failed to meet Khial's expectations. She squared her shoulders. "You're going to say it's too soon. Or that it's impossible for us to be together."

Khial regarded her from across the bed, Dain lying peacefully between them. "I knew that Dain was my mate at first sight." He mirrored her squared stance. "As for impossible to be together?"

Khial paused. She hadn't run thus far. Not from Dain's grasping family, whom she'd have to now contend with if she got with an heir. She didn't run from Dain's illness. If she didn't run from this last piece to their warped puzzle, Khial just might have to give to her, her fair due.

"I'm fairly certain my mother had Dain's parents killed. That is after she drove my fathers to kill one another."

Chanyn's eyes went owl-wide, but her feet stayed rooted.

"My mother was the last descendant of the royal family of the Africas. Most of my life I've seen people look at me out of the sides of their eyes, wondering when I'll snap like she did." He gazed down at the man who never cut him a side eye. "Her blood is my blood. Whatever madness she was born with runs through me. Yet every night, he sleeps soundly in my arms." Khial stood silent, waiting for Chanyn's response.

"So, that makes you a prince?"

Khial laughed at the unexpected remark.

Chanyn grinned.

Dain stirred.

They both waited in silence until Dain settled. Then Khial considered the Lady Chanyn once more. "You don't scare easily, do you?"

"What should I be scared of? Each of our parents made bad choices. None of us are following in their footsteps. I can see that you don't like me, but I don't think you would harm me."

Her look at him was defiant, as though she challenged him to prove her wrong. And finally, Khial gave up the battle to dislike this strong, proud creature.

"In answer to your first question," he said, "I think that anything's possible. Maybe you and your monk can have your happily-ever-after one day."

"You don't want me, do you?"

Khial looked at the proud tilt to her chin. Her arms crossed over her chest, plumping up those full breasts. The nipples pointing right at him, shining a light on the truth hardening in his pants. He saw a hint of thigh at the slit in her dress. Finally, he looked back into her eyes.

"You're right. I don't want you in the bond," he said. "I resent you trying to step in and be the hero to my love story."

She surprised him again by nodding in understanding. "I don't want to disrupt your story, Khial. But I do want to help. Dain's my friend. He's my only friend. I don't want him to die. But if that can't be helped, I want to grant whatever his wishes are."

"I don't care about his money."

"Neither, do I."

They paused and regarded each other from opposite sides of the bed.

"So, what are we going to do?" she asked.

Khial shrugged. He'd been trying to puzzle that out since before she got here a week ago. He was no closer to an answer of his own. She was going to have to come to her own conclusions.

"Why don't you have a talk with your monk. He'll be here tonight."

CHAPTER THREE

IT STILL SURPRISED JIAN THAT he was received into the house. The manservant, he'd learned his name was Rianald, gave Jian a slight bow of deference. As a third son, receiving the deference of a bow was something he never thought possible. Only his eldest brother, the first-born son and thereby lord, obtained that respect.

Jian had seen his eldest brother a few times walking the street. The two men could have been twins, they so resembled each other. The one time Jian left the temple without his robes, that time he went to her to run away and elope, he'd been mistaken for his brother.

At the time, Jian thought it a sign. A good sign. He would be accepted into polite society after his bonding. Perhaps he would walk the streets with his brother instead of his brother pretending not to know the man with whom he shared a face and blood. Later that fateful day, Jian trudged back to the temple covered in mud. The same people, who earlier recognized him as his brother, gasped and then burst into laughter, pointing and jeering.

It was the last day anyone bowed to him.

Rianald straightened and let Jian pass. "Lady Chanyn is in her room, Brother Jian."

Jian made his way up the staircase. He adjusted the folds of his robes, ran a hand down the planes of his shaved head, and licked his dry lips. He felt watched.

On the wall hung a portrait, a radiant blonde woman embraced by two equally blonde males. Lord Dain's parents, three of a small number of erotic artists. The portrait hung high on the wall, out of reach, much like their performances. You could look, you could imagine, you could yearn, but you couldn't touch Lady Darlyn.

At Chanyn's door, Jian hesitated. His hand paused in the process of forming a fist to knock. He lowered his hand and took a step back. Jian leaned his back to the opposite wall and stared at the door.

He'd spent the last forty-eight hours in silent meditation, praying for clarity, for strength. He would go for long stretches of peace, but then Chanyn's name or her face would pop into his mind and his heart would rend.

He'd given her time to think things through. She was a smart woman. She would come to the best decision for herself. She would accept Lord Dain's proposal and agree to conceive his heir. The decision would put her in the best possible position, one of wealth and security. It was that particular thought, the thought of Chanyn being cared for and comfortable, that set his soul at ease. It made him happy, prideful even, that he would have something to do with putting her in that position.

Still, he dreaded crossing the threshold and watching, hearing, her take back her affections in exchange for the comfort they both wanted for her. The last time a woman withdrew her declaration of love he hadn't been standing face to face with her. This time he had to stand up like a man and take the rejection. It was a high price. One he knew needed to be paid in order for Chanyn to have a life of ease.

"She thinks she's in love with you."

Jian turned to see Lord Khial striding toward him. Dressed in a cream shirt that opened to reveal the rich mahogany of his chiseled chest. The man moved like a cat. A seductive grace that hinted at quick strength.

Jian straightened away from the wall. "I'm not going to run away with her, if that's what you think."

Lord Khial shrugged. "I wouldn't stop you."

That was not the answer Jian expected. His eyes narrowed in suspicion. "She believes you do not like her."

Lord Khial's stoney face cracked into a grin. "I didn't, but we've come to an understanding."

Jian averted his eyes from that mischievous grin. Of course they had. They were both about to become very wealthy with the imminent demise of Lord Dain.

As though reading his mind, Lord Khial said, "I'm not after his money."

Jian could believe that of Lord Khial, he knew the man descended from royalty and wealth.

"Neither is she," Lord Khial continued.

"Everyone wants comfort, be it money or family."

"Even you, monk?"

"I have family," Jian said. "My brothers at the temple. They took me in."

"You're a third? Your family discarded you?"

The term never failed to rankle. "Yes, my mother gave me up." Jian's mother turned him out of the house at the age of twelve. Once a male child reached twelve, he could be legally cast out without repercussions from the Sisterhood.

Khial placed his back to the wall and regarded Chanyn's door. "My mother liked to measure my emotional and mental responses to different stimuli. Once, she told me I was technically a third, because she'd had two miscarriages. So, she cast me out. It was only for two weeks, and only to the back woods of the family estate. She was testing the theory of nature versus nurture. She wanted to find out if my base human instincts would help me survive or would my nurtured upbringing cause me to perish."

Lord Khial paused, detached, but still lost in memory. "I was five years old at the time."

Jian's hand reached out on instinct, but he caught himself just in time before making contact with the young lord. He'd heard the tales of Lord Khial's mother. A descendant of royalty, a great beauty, and an intellectual who did many controversial, but groundbreaking, studies on the human mind. She was also the only woman in recent history serving a sentence for second-degree murder. Her final experiment caused her bondmates to kill each other in a fit of rage. Rage she'd stirred within them.

"She couldn't feel empathy," Lord Khial continued. "Sociopath, is what the disorder is called. It wasn't her worst experiment. Dain was born with a weak heart but his mother willed him to live with her love alone. I spent my childhood as a human lab rat. Chanyn spent hers in isolation with a neglectful mother. And you were discarded by yours. I can't blame any of us for seeking comfort where we can find it."

Lord Khial's face molded to stone once more. He pushed off the wall, but then he paused, looking at Chanyn's door. He turned and leveled a glare on Jian. "Do not upset her." Lord Khial's own vehemence must've surprised him because his expression cracked, just slightly. "Dain wouldn't like it."

He turned to go, but paused at the sound of Jian's voice.

"Anger is a weather system."

"What?" Lord Khial scowled, turning back.

"It's something my mentor taught me. Anger is like a weather system. It has heat and pressure. Its winds are righteousness. But at the eye of the storm are fear and powerlessness."

"Don't try to psychoanalyze me monk. I survived the best."

"That's my point, my lord. You're not the system," Jian said. "You're a tree. You stood stubbornly in the wind and it made you strong. But the system has moved on. You can let your guard down."

Lord Khial's blue eyes were as cold as granite before he turned and walked on.

Jian gathered his courage and knocked on the door.

"Come in," Chanyn called.

She sat in a chair, clothed in a modest day dress. She didn't stand.

"Lady Chanyn," Jian bowed.

"Hi," she said from her perch.

He straightened and dared to look at her, and then almost fell to his knees. She had been crying; the red around her eyes evident. The liquid gold churned. Her mouth was set in a determined line, her chin lifted.

"My friend is dying," she said. "My mother died a few months ago.

I didn't cry when I found her lying still. I had to dig her grave and carry her out of our home, far enough away so that animals wouldn't come near our home after me. And then I was all alone."

Jian did go to her then. The thought of Chanyn being alone nearly killed him. He took her hands in his own. She looked down at their entwined fingers and gave them a squeeze as though to test their realness.

"I've only known Dain for a week and he's not even gone yet. But here I am crying over his death. Our connection, and the care that we share for each other, is real. What I feel for my friend is real. It hurts and you can see the evidence of the pain in my tears."

She wiped at her face and continued. "I've known you for less time than I've known Dain. Our connection, what we shared with each other and the care that we have for one another are also real. I know it is."

Jian's heart pounded in its cage, begging to be free to speak.

"I'm going to conceive a child with my friend," Chanyn continued. "I'm doing it because he thinks it will save me and the love of his life. I'm doing it because he has given me so much and this is the only thing he's asked of me. But I need to understand why you're doing it, Jian?"

Jian swallowed. Chanyn held his gaze. He knew he should look away from her. Everything would show plainly on his face. She would see it all if he didn't look away. She'd see his heart beating in the reflection of his eyes. She'd see the desire to bring her close in his eyes. She'd see the desire to protect her in his eyes. She'd see his very soul yearning to join with her if he didn't look away right now.

Jian managed to blink. In the instant of that blink and his lids reopening, it was too late. When Jian focused once more on Chanyn, he saw the bright light of hope in her eyes.

"Chanyn," he sighed. He could close his eyes now. He shut them tight and bowed his head into her lap. She ran her fingers over his brow and Jian was nearly lost. Nearly.

He stayed in her lap as he spoke. "You say Lord Dain's friendship means the world to you. My brothers at the temple mean the world to me. They have given me so much, also asking little in return."

Jian straightened. This part of the story had to be told face to face.

"Five years ago, I trained a woman, a young girl, really. She was newly eighteen, newly mated. She believed herself in love with me. I wanted to believe it too. You know that only first sons are allowed to bond. I am a third and a monk at that. I took a vow to serve the Goddess in her temple for all my days. But I threw it all away on the whim of a girl who didn't know the meaning of love, or the devotion and sacrifice that comes with it. She came to her senses when she realized we would be penniless.

"She went on to bond with her two mates. All was forgiven for her. But for me, my temple was ostracized by the scandal. My brothers nearly starved because of my folly. I can't do that to them again. Even if this time it's..."

He didn't dare complete that sentence. He began another.

"Your pleasure has given me such happiness. A happiness that I never expected to know. A man cannot serve two mistresses. I cannot stay with you. Before I go, I want to give you the family that neither of us has had. I believe you will make the greatest mother. If you will allow me to be a part of your conception and secure your future it will fill my heart for the rest of my days."

Chanyn sat silent for a moment, eyes boring into his, peering into his soul. "You believe that what I feel for you is real?"

Jian hesitated, but then nodded.

"I believe that you feel the same way," she said.

Jian closed his eyes and willed his head and heart to remain still.

When he opened his eyes, she held her arms wide before him.

For a moment, Jian didn't comprehend. He'd never been offered a hug before. He'd been embraced in the throes of passion. But no one had ever held their arms out to him for the sole purpose of comforting him. He went tentatively into her arms. Once they made contact, he engulfed her, holding her firmly against his body. They stayed that way for many moments.

Chanyn sighed deeply. He felt the weariness in her bones. He lifted her and carried her to the bed. Lying down beside her, he brought her once more into his arms. She settled her head on his chest.

After some time she spoke. "I wouldn't ask you to give up your family, Jian. Just as I know you won't ask me to forsake my friend. All my life I've only wanted one thing, and after the last time we were together I thought it had slipped through my fingers. I refuse to have any more regrets in this life. So if you won't say it, I will."

And then she did.

They were just three little words, but they took him to a soul-peaceful place meditation had never once achieved for him.

CHAPTER FOUR

CHANYN LOOKED DOWN AT THE gold band on her finger. The array of jewels winked back at her. The gold bonded her to Dain and Khial. On the band sparkled three gems. The ruby was Dain's pledge, the sapphire Khial's. The diamond at the center was a tradition held over from the twentieth century. It held no meaning other than decorative. Women didn't need to pledge anything to men. The third gem was simply a symbol of status. Rianald told her that the larger the diamond the more wealthy the woman. Chanyn's diamond was huge.

She was married.

The ceremony had been lavish, but brief. She had to do nothing but walk out in a lovely gown of white. She looked virginal, innocent, naive. That would have been true a week ago, but it was no longer. Chanyn knew that the people who shared your blood could be callous and devious. She knew that life could take the worst and put power in their hands, and then take the best and put weakness in their hearts. Chanyn itched to take the gown off, but the night was far from over.

The crowded ceremonial hall held more people than she'd seen in her entire life. People coming to gape at the wildling found outside the city walls, no doubt. Lump that in with the spectacle of being bound to two of the city's most notorious sons. There were a good deal of gasps, a few snickers, but mostly they just stared.

Rianald, Tem, and Brent outdid themselves on Chanyn's hair and makeup. Her gown showed all her best features, lifting her breasts and accentuating her hips. Her hair was a soft halo around her head. Her make up took her own breath away when she looked in the mirror. The onlookers may have come to gape, but Dain's manservants made sure they left envious.

She was married.

She had to keep repeating it to herself just to make it true.

She was married. It was nothing like she'd dreamed. First, she was married to two men. Second, neither of them were her true love. One of her husbands she felt a deep kinship to, while she shared a speculative truce with the other. The man she loved hadn't even come to her wedding. But at least one of her relatives had.

At the end of the ceremony, as Chanyn, Dain, and Khial took the felicitations of well-wishers, Merlyn made her way to Chanyn. A handsome young man with red hair, green eyes and golden skin trailed behind her.

"Greetings cousin," Merlyn said. "I bring glad tidings from our family."

Chanyn's shoulders jerked in surprise. "Really?"

Merlyn hesitated and then shook her head once. "No," she admitted. "But custom dictates that when a family member is bonded they should have representatives from their family as witnesses."

Merlyn recited the facts as though she read them from a book. Her speech pattern reminding Chanyn of her mother's. What differentiated Merlyn from Chanyn's mother was the hint of compassion in her eyes.

"So, because of custom," Merlyn lifted a delicate shoulder not quite meeting Chanyn's eyes, "here I am. I wouldn't want your bond made illegitimate on a technicality."

Chanyn reached out a hand to Merlyn's shoulder. "That was very kind of you."

Merlyn stared at Chanyn's hand. Chanyn pulled her hand back, afraid she'd broken some custom. Chanyn's mother hadn't liked any forms of touch and Chanyn frequently forgot to keep her hands to herself despite years of admonishments.

Chanyn glanced over Merlyn's shoulder. "Who's your friend?"

Merlyn followed Chanyn's glance. "Oh, that's just Liam. He's my betrothed." Merlyn threw out the comment casually.

Chanyn held out her hand to the young man. "It's nice to meet you, Liam."

Liam looked at Chanyn's hand in utter shock.

"Whatever are you doing?" asked Merlyn, her head cocked to the side like a bird's.

Chanyn pulled her offensive hand away, cradling it to her heart. "I was greeting my soon to be cousin-in-law."

Both Merlyn and Liam stared at her. Off to the side Chanyn could see Dain grinning good-humoredly in her direction. She raised her brows high as though to say, What have I done wrong now? Though she couldn't hear it, she saw Dain's chest tremble with a chuckle. Chanyn couldn't help but note how well he looked after a couple of days rest.

"I think you might be as feral as grandmother says you are."

What did she have to lose? Chanyn leaned in conspiratorially. "I think you might be right."

Merlyn blinked, and then laughed. The sound seemed to startle her and she took a moment to collect herself. A small grin remained as she looked once more at Chanyn. With Merlyn's face relaxed she saw the family resemblance, the high cheekbones and full lips, the same brown-gold inquisitive eyes as Chanyn's reflection.

But then Merlyn's face sobered. "I hear you're being trained by a Pleasure Hound." She whispered the words Pleasure Hound as though they were some sort of obscenity.

Chanyn nodded. Merlyn stepped in closer.

"I used to know a hound," Merlyn confided. "Well he wasn't a hound when I knew him. He used to work on the estate. But then there was an... incident."

Over Merlyn's shoulder, Chanyn saw Liam bristle. His shoulders stiffened and his jaw clenched.

"He was sent away. He entered the pleasure temple sometime after that." Merlyn wouldn't meet Chanyn's eyes as she continued. "I don't suppose you know him?"

"My hound's name is Jian." Her hound. If only.

"Oh," Merlyn's face relaxed. "That's not him. In any case, good luck on your wedding night. I have heard that with a hound present it won't be as unpleasant." Merlyn ran an envious gaze over Chanyn. "It once was the accepted custom for a newly bonded triad to employ the services of a hound. Grand Mother would never allow a hound near any of her daughters. She believes males should never have any control over a female."

"Our mothers didn't love our fathers?"

Merlyn blinked, her expression uncertain as though she were trying to determine if Chanyn made a joke or stated a fact. "Oh, Chanyn," she said finally. "You say the most peculiar things. All the women in our family had mates selected using a very scientific process. Grand Mother does a complete genealogical study to determine male intelligence and obedience. Once she finds my second mate, I'll be bonded and expected to breed. But," and now she came in closer to Chanyn, closer than custom dictated. "I have a theory that a child's gender is determined by the male sperm. All men come from women. Therefore, they contain both male and female DNA, where women only contain the female. So it should follow that it's the man's sperm that determines the sex of the fetus. There were studies done back in the twentieth, but most of that information has been lost or destroyed. But I think I'm close to cracking the code. I hope to complete my work before Grand Mother finds me a second mate. I'm certain a pregnancy would slow me down."

Chanyn glanced again at the male at Merlyn's back. He hadn't spoken a word. He met her eyes. His dark gaze reminded Chanyn of the boar she'd slain in front of Dain and Khial. The creature had only been seeking warmth. When it found a place it thought safe, it had been gutted.

"I would like to see you again," Merlyn said, suddenly shy. "Though I don't think that Grand Mother would approve."

"You're welcome to come over at any time."

Delight shone in Merlyn's eyes. She reached out a tentative hand and patted Chanyn's shoulder in an approximation of the gesture Chanyn had done earlier.

Merlyn turned to go, but then stopped and turned back. "They're not all bad. Our family. They want what's best for us. They don't waste time with... emotions like love. Or friendship."

"I'd like to be your friend," Chanyn said. "If that's agreeable to you."

Merlyn beamed, then quickly composed herself. She turned to go. Liam regarded Chanyn with a quirk of a brow. Chanyn offered him a friendly smile, but he looked away and followed close behind Merlyn.

Dain came over to her then. "Are you ready to go, my lady?"

Ready to go to her wedding night. With her husbands, and her hound.

Chanyn hadn't seen Jian since the night he held her after she professed her love for him. Chanyn had said the words out loud, but Jian hadn't. He hadn't needed to. His heart was in every look, every touch, every kiss.

He'd held her all night, neither of them needing any further physical connection than lying in each other's embrace. In the morning he'd waited for her to awaken before kissing her lightly, like she were the most precious thing in the world, and then leaving.

The next two days had been a blur of preparations for the ceremony, followed by quiet evenings sitting with Dain, and sometimes Khial, as Dain recovered.

Now Chanyn took her husband's hand as they left the bonding temple and returned home to consummate the bond. Khial trailed behind them.

CHAPTER FIVE

THREE SMALL GEMS WINKED BACK at Khial in mockery when he looked down at the band on his finger. There was his family stone, the sapphire. The stone meant loyalty to family and healthy relationships. Khial clenched his fists so he wouldn't wrench the lie off his finger. The band bit into his hand.

His thumb traced over the ruby. The feel of Dain's stone instantly calmed him. The red stone was a promise that Khial never felt necessary to publicize. Between the lie, and the promise, sat the sparkling diamond that represented their wife.

Khial was married. To the man he'd pledged his life to as a boy, and to a woman he barely knew as a man.

The last two days he and Chanyn had been cordial. Their goals were in alignment, with each nursing Dain back to health. Thumbing their noses at his weak organ, willing Dain's heart to keep beating just as his mother and fathers had kept it beating with only the force of their love. Khial believed that he and Chanyn could do the same for him.

Today, Dain looked the picture of health. A perspiring picture of health. An anxious picture of health. A slightly trembling picture of health.

"You don't have to do this," Khial said.

Dain wiped the sweat from his brow with a clenched fist and thrust up his chin. Khial sighed at the stubbornness of his mate, his husband. He sighed to keep from laughing. The action brought to mind a young Dain fearful of jumping off a cliff into a stream of water.

"You don't have to do this," Khial had yelled up at him then, while he tread water below the cliff.

The younger Dain had thrust his chin out in the same way as his older self. He'd taken a deep breath, and jumped. At the bottom, in the cool water, the two had laughed and splashed each other. It had been a high jump and not the best of dares for a sickly child. But Khial knew that if Dain had hurt himself on the fall, he would have been right there to catch him. Khial would always be there to catch Dain.

They stood before the marital suite once occupied by Dain's parents. They'd never used this room. Dain's rooms were large enough to suite them both. But, now that there were three of them...

Dain reached out a hand to Khial's shoulder. "You have been a part of my family for as long as I can remember. Just as my parents embraced you, I need you to embrace her. She is a part of our family now."

Khial looked into those green eyes that he woke up to every morning, and the last thing he saw before he went to sleep each night. Dain was healthy. He would stay healthy. Khial had to admit that part of Dain's recovery was due to Chanyn. With her second pair of hands added to his, Dain recovered in half the time. That fact should have made Khial bitter, but it didn't. It couldn't, when he looked into Dain's healthy, determined face. Khial felt nothing but gratitude for Chanyn's care and help.

"I'll embrace her as family," Khial acquiesced, "but not as anything else."

Khial passed in front of Dain, anxious to get this night over. He was not enthused about watching his lover make love to another person. At least that's what he told himself. His dick, on the other hand, throbbed at the thoughts he refused to have about the ordeal. He refused to remember Chanyn's glistening skin, her chocolate dipped nipples, her parted lips...

Khial turned the handle.

On the other side of the door, Chanyn sat on the bed, fully clothed, though the silk covering her was scant. Alongside her sat the monk. When Khial opened the door, he spied their entwined hands, heads bent together in an intimate conversation. At Khial's entrance, the monk's fingers loosened on Chanyn's, but as his eyes connected with Khial's, Khial saw the monk change his mind. He re-clasped his hands with Chanyn's and brought them both to standing. They looked like a united front.

For a moment, Khial wondered if the monk was going to go back on his word. Were they about to tell Khial and Dain that they were running away together?

Dain came in behind Khial.

The monk released one of Chanyn's hands and bowed to both Dain and Khial. "Greetings, my lords, and felicitations on your bonding."

Khial followed Dain's eyes to the entwined hands of their wife and the monk, but Dain didn't say anything about it. "Thank you Brother Jian. Is our lady prepared?"

After his grand speech just a moment ago, Khial heard the nervousness return to Dain's voice. Khial glanced over at Chanyn. He saw a tremble in her free hand. It appeared the only two people in the room who weren't trembling or nervous were Khial and the monk.

"We are ready, my lord," the monk spoke for Chanyn. "Will you join us in prayer?" The monk reached a hand towards Dain. Dain stepped up and took it.

They all looked expectantly at Khial. He looked at the circle of people: the man he loved, his wife, and the man she loved.

"I won't be joining in," said Khial. He went to the window, turning his back to the whole affair. The joke was on him. He could clearly see them all in the glass' reflection. Khial stood on the outside looking in as Dain and Chanyn clasped hands with the monk and closed the circle.

The monk began his prayer.

"Maternal Goddess, I seek your presence as I align myself with one of your sacred daughters.

I offer my body as a vessel of your will and your grace.

The desire of my heart is pure and known to you.

I wish to please your daughter and garner your favor.

The miracle that pleases a woman and creates life is of your design, Divine Goddess.

With great anticipation, I align all of the energy systems of my body, my soul, and my mind with you.

I give thanks in advance for your blessings of this experience and know that I walk in the light of your sun and the fertility of your earth.

Ashe."

"Ashe," intoned Chanyn and Dain.

They stood silently, eyes closed, heads bowed in meditation. Then the monk took Chanyn's hand and moved her towards the bed. The monk's back was to Dain so he couldn't see the questioning look he gave Chanyn. From the reflection of the glass, Khial saw Chanyn answer the monk with a trusting nod.

The monk pulled the ties of her gown and the material fell to the ground. Khial heard Dain gasp. Khial had seen Chanyn before, but still his fingers gripped the windowsill as he beheld her once more. She'd been sitting the last time Khial saw her so he hadn't seen how perfectly proportioned she was. Large breasts, small waist, flaring hips and the triangle of curls below her navel. Khial had to swallow many times. His dick throbbed, begging him to turn around.

Khial closed his eyes and heard the bed creak indicating Chanyn climbed aboard.

"No, no," came the monk's gentle voice. "Do not disrobe just yet, my lord. We must prepare her."

"I thought you said she was ready?" Dain's voice was husky.

"I said she is prepared, my lord. We have to make her ready. A man may become aroused in an instant. That is not so with a woman. Come, let me show you."

Khial's senses were so aware that he heard Dain move closer to the bed. A moment later, he heard Chanyn's small sigh.

"You're doing very well, my lord," encouraged the monk. "Only, a woman needs a slower, lighter touch. Like this."

Chanyn let out something between a groan and a sigh. Khial could take it no longer. He opened his eyes and gaped at the reflection in the window.

Chanyn lay on the bed, Dain and the monk on either side of her, their hands gliding over her body. Khial saw Chanyn undulating under their touch. He clenched his hands once more.

The monk's eyes roamed over and caught Khial's eyes in the glass. The monk held Khial there as he continued moving his hands over Chanyn's body. Khial looked away from the monk's eyes and followed his hands as they went over Chanyn's breasts. Then Khial's eyes went back to the monk. The monk still looked at Khial's reflection in the window. He said nothing, his face a mask of serenity.

"Now you may disrobe, my lord."

Khial's hand slipped off the window ledge from all the sweat gathered on his palm. The monk tore his gaze from Khial and his eyes landed on Dain. It had to be Khial's imagination. The monk did not just smirk at Khial before turning his serene face to Dain.

Dain straightened, his fingers trembling once more.

Dain made quick work of his clothes and then stood before both Chanyn and the monk in all his naked glory. The throbbing of Khial's dick became nearly unbearable now.

The monk slid behind Chanyn, sitting her up and cradling her in his arms. Khial saw him smile down at her, the look both supportive and an acknowledgement of love. It was that exchange, and not the fact that his bond mate and wife stood naked preparing to couple, that made Khial feel like a voyeur. He nearly looked away, but when Dain climbed on the bed and between Chanyn's thighs, Khial had had enough.

He turned around.

Dain had his dick in hand. He slowly approached Chanyn who had her legs spread. Khial saw the dark pink of her. He swallowed, fingertips still gripping the windowsill behind him.

"Enter her as slowly as possible," the monk instructed.

Dain nodded, focused exclusively on his target. Lining himself up, he began to push. The head of Dain's dick disappeared and his eyes went wide.

"Slowly," said the monk. "The first time can be..."

While the monk searched for an adjective, Dain gave another push. His mouth gaped open. His dick disappeared inside Chanyn.

Chanyn stiffened.

Dain let out a guttural roar as his body began to jerk.

The monk found the adjective to describe Dain's new experience. "...overwhelming."

It took Dain a moment to recover. Chanyn and the monk waited patiently. The monk stroked Chanyn's arm and back. Chanyn patted Dain on his shoulders. Finally, Dain regained sense and withdrew from her. Chanyn winced as he did so.

Dain looked horrified. "I'm so sorry, Chanyn." He came up to kneeling, his dick soft after the overwhelming impact.

Chanyn folded her legs away from him. "You didn't hurt me."

Dain looked away, shamefaced. "Well, at least it's done now."

"No," said the monk as he continued to stroke Chanyn's arm. "It is not."

Both Khial and Dain gaped at the monk.

"She needs to experience orgasm in order for conception, particularly for the conception of a female child."

Dain looked down at his dick, limp and lazy.

"Lord Khial?"

It took Khial a moment to remember that that was his name.

"Would you help your bond mate?" The monk cocked his head in Dain's direction.

Khial looked from the monk to Dain. "Help him?"

"Yes," the monk answered patiently. "He needs to achieve another erection."

Slowly the words and their meaning became clear to Khial. With a stiff arm, he pushed himself away from the windowsill. The first step felt as though he were going off a cliff. Khial kept his eyes on Dain. On shaky legs, he let go of the ledge and made his way down the cliff towards his lover.

CHAPTER SIX

JIAN OBSERVED LORD KHIAL PERFORM a death march to the bed, his face shell-shocked at Jian's request to rouse his bond mate for a second go. In truth, it would have been easier if Lord Khial were a willing partner; the man was certainly able at the moment. That erection Jian spied between his legs must be killing him.

Lord Khial arrived at the other side of the bed. He stood before Lord Dain, unsure what to do next. Finally, Lord Dain reached up to him.

"You know that I love you, Khi. You don't doubt that."

Lord Khial glanced at Chanyn, who was curled up in Jian's arms watching the exchange. Jian told her that the first time with her husbands might go this way. She had been prepared. Lord Dain did well at getting her ready, though Jian knew that it would not have happened without his instruction. It was largely Jian's touch that Chanyn responded to.

Jian expected to feel jealousy, bitterness, at the evening's events. But neither sinful emotion reared within him. He knew his actions tonight would secure the future of the woman who held his heart. He would have stood in front of a brute squad to ensure her happiness. Instead, he got to orchestrate her pleasure.

He saw that Lord Dain did indeed care for Chanyn. He believed that Lord Khial would never harm her. Once Lord Khial's grief at the loss of Lord Dain left him, he would protect Chanyn and their child. The display in the hall the other week hadn't fooled Jian. The young lord carried a tender spot for Chanyn, even if he wasn't ready to admit it to himself.

Lord Khial's eyes lifted to Chanyn. Jian saw some silent agreement pass between them. Whatever Lord Khial saw there decided him. He nodded to Lord Dain and then sank to his knees.

The two men kissed, tentatively. Jian was certain neither of them had ever had an audience to their lovemaking before. He turned his attention back to Chanyn and brought her head around.

"Hi," he said, mimicking her greeting from the other day.

"Hi."

They looked at each other for a moment, each grinning.

"This time," Jian said, "I promise you pleasure."

Chanyn relaxed her head deeper into the cradle of his shoulder. Her eyes so full of faith and certainty that it nearly knocked Jian back.

"I trust you, Jian." She pulled his head down.

At first Jian went willingly. He'd missed the feel of her lips on his. But as she stroked his top lip with her tongue, Jian froze, remembering that they too had an audience. His eyes sought her husbands.

Lord Dain's eyes were closed, his head resting on Lord Khial's shoulders. Jian couldn't see from this angle, but he knew Lord Khial stroked his mate. Lord Khial's eyes were on Jian and Chanyn.

The two men regarded each other as they continued to pleasure the lovers in their embraces. Years ago, when words of love had been whispered to Jian, they were done in secret, behind closed doors, hidden. Chanyn didn't hide her feelings for him. Even now, in front of her two husbands, Chanyn's feelings for Jian were not a quiet secret. They were fully on display, a proud declaration.

Lord Khial's scrutiny held no judgment. His expression marked Jian as a welcome partner in this room, albeit a temporary one.

Jian heard Lord Dain's breathing change.

"Is he ready?"

Lord Khial nodded. He stood and took a step away, but Lord Dain reached out a hand.

"Stay with me," Lord Dain pleaded. After a second's hesitation, Lord Khial slowly released a breath and planted his feet.

Lord Dain kneeled on the bed before Chanyn once more.

With his arms still around her, Jian leaned down and whispered in her ear. "I've got you." He felt her internal sigh. Any remaining tension released from her body as she sank back into him with complete trust and surrender.

Jian looked to Lord Dain. "Slowly this time."

The man nodded.

Jian let Chanyn's torso rest against his chest and then he opened her thighs to her husband. Her scent was heady. All male eyes drew to the core of her. Jian heard the other two males gulp the scent down. Lord Dain's shaft visibly throbbed, veins pulsating, precum at the head. The man wasn't going to last any longer the second time.

Lord Khial stared transfixed at Chanyn's core. The man had feigned disinterest only to be held rapt by the mere reflection of the bed sport.

"Lord Khial, I'll need your help."

Lord Khial's eyes locked on Jian's, that sea blue going wide with trepidation.

"I'll need you to hold on to Lord Dain's testicles."

A gulf of confusion spread across Lord Khial's face.

"It will help stall his climax until we can get Lady Chanyn's orgasm underway."

Lord Khial took in a slow breath. He slipped off his shoes and came onto the bed behind Lord Dain.

"Let's begin," said Jian.

Lord Dain entered Chanyn slowly. He panted as he fully seated himself inside her. He brought both arms to rest on either side of Chanyn's torso.

Jian nodded to Lord Khial, who braced one hand on his mate's back, the other disappeared below to grasp Lord Dain's testicles. Lord Dain gasped.

"You'll need to hold them a little tighter than you would in normal lovemaking." Jian thought he saw Lord Khial wince in embarrassment. He had to stop himself from smiling at the man's shyness.

Everyone was nearly in place. Jian placed his second and third fingers into his mouth to wet them. Then he placed the moist digits onto Chanyn's clitoris. She gasped.

"Move," Jian told Lord Dain.

And he did.

Immediately, Jian felt Chanyn swelling against his fingers. Her climax was imminent. The shuddering impact of her inner muscles could easily pull Lord Dain under.

"Hold him tighter," Jian said to Lord Khial.

Lord Khial stared raptly at the joining of his mates. Jian had to call the man's name again and repeat his instructions. It wasn't too soon, because Chanyn began to tremble.

As her climax took her, she pulled Jian's head down to hers. He caught her cries in a kiss, his fingers never ceasing on her slippery heat. He delved into her mouth stroking her tongue as her husband stroked into her core.

Finally, they broke apart, in need of air. Chanyn's eyes were closed, still riding the ecstasy of one man inside her, another on her bud, and still another at the rear. Jian knew that Lord Khial's position had his hand grazing Chanyn's rear every now and again. Ever the teacher, Jian made a note that she would likely enjoy double-penetration. Not all women did.

When Jian glanced up he was met with two sets of gaping male eyes. At first he couldn't understand what the matter was. Then he realized, he'd kissed their wife, passionately. Most bonded triads didn't engage in kissing. Sex was viewed with one sole purpose in this day and age: to beget children, namely girls. Not many women cared to experience the pleasure of kissing.

Jian couldn't muster any shame. He'd done his duty. The lady writhed in pleasure under his touch, his mouth. He raised his chin in defiance.

Lord Khial voiced no objections. If Lord Dain had any they weren't voiced either as he closed his eyes and got lost once more in the pleasure of the bonding with his wife.

"I'd like her to have two more orgasms before we're finished," Jian said. He barely had Lord Dain's attention, so he directed his instructions to Lord Khial. "I'm going to tilt her hips. Lord Dain will need to come off his forearms. Can you manage that?"

Lord Khial kept one hand low on Dain's sack to stay his mate's orgasm, then wrapped the other arm around Lord Dain's chest, bringing him flush against his back. Lord Dain went willingly, one arm snaking behind to embrace Lord Khial.

Jian lifted Chanyn's hips and all three of them gasped.

Jian knew Lady Chanyn gasped at the change in angle of penetration. This angle would hit a bundle of tissues at the front of her pelvis. Unlike a woman's clitoris, this spot could handle multiple orgasms in a short span of time.

Jian knew from experience that Lord Dain gasped because the change in angle made a woman's core grip him tighter.

Jian suspected Lord Khial gasped as his lover's rear came into contact with his swollen shaft each time he withdrew from Chanyn.

The room filled with the sounds of pleasure. Pleasure that was all Jian's manipulation. He felt well pleased with himself. This was why he did this work. The art of sex, when done right, was an ode to the Goddess, a benediction of Her divine will.

Jian could tell he wasn't going to get Chanyn to a third orgasm. All three of the bonded mates were fast approaching a grand climax.

Jian spoke to Lord Khial. "Let his testicles go, but hold his torso tight."

Lord Khial nodded, his eyes dazed. The man might deny his own need, but it would come if Jian kept him involved in the sacrament.

"Let him know," Jian said to Lord Khial, "that you want him to come. Keep telling him."

Lord Khial could only get every other word out to his mate. Both males' eyes were pleasure glazed, their breaths quick. Lord Dain turned his head and kissed Khial deeply.

Jian turned his attention to his own heart. Chanyn watched the men, enraptured.

"They're so beautiful," she whispered.

Jian leaned down and kissed her temple. "I want you to come for me, Chanyn."

As soon as the words left his mouth she began to tremble in his arms. Once more he captured her cries with his mouth, telling her over and over again how much she meant to him with his tongue. He heard the other men climaxing, but his attention didn't waver from her. He rained kisses down over her face until her breathing returned to a semblance of normal.

When he looked up, he met Lord Khial's eyes. The other man did the same, he rained kisses down the side of his lover's face.

Jian nodded to him with respect. "Ashe."

CHAPTER SEVEN

DARKNESS REIGNED OUTSIDE THE WINDOWS when Chanyn opened her eyes, but it wasn't hard to see in the dim room. The solar lights, though full of gathered energy from the day, were now dimmed. Her eyes met a hairless chest. The forearm that belonged to the chest made up and down motions. She felt the maneuvers on her back. She didn't want to move, but she wanted to see Jian's eyes. She tilted her head up.

Jian stared at the ceiling. The lines of his face relaxed, peaceful. His eyes darted quickly here and then there, lost in thought. Sensing her attention, his gaze turned to Chanyn and he smiled. It caught Chanyn's breath. He'd never smiled at her unprovoked. This smile he gave to her freely.

"Hi," she said.

"How are you feeling, my lady?"

There was a bit of soreness between her thighs. It was the first time she'd felt sore there. After the first time with Jian she had only felt a pleasant fullness. Thinking on that night alone with Jian brought the happenings of last night, actually still this night, back to the forefront of Chanyn's mind.

"Where are Dain and Khial?"

Jian rolled Chanyn fully onto her back and came over top of her. His chest, in his open robes, met her naked breasts. "The activities of the night exerted Lord Dain."

Chanyn's eyes widened. If Dain were ill, she needed to go to him. She made a move to get up.

"He's fine," Jian assured her. "But Lord Khial thought it best if they retire to their own room so that you both could rest in peace."

For a moment disappointment crept into Chanyn's heart. They didn't include her in the decision. She was a part of their bond now. But then she realized that their decision afforded her more time alone with Jian. She wasn't sure how much time she would have with him before she became pregnant and they had to part ways permanently.

Chanyn relaxed under him. Though she was a bit sore, she still wanted him. They hadn't made love since that first time over a week ago. He'd only held her and fallen asleep with her in his arms a few nights back. And though it was the best night she'd ever experienced, she wanted to feel him and him alone inside her.

Chanyn reached up to caress his face. Jian covered her hand with his, regret on his brows. He closed his eyes and kissed her palm. Then he turned from her and rose from the bed. Chanyn didn't like the distance he put between them.

"I've run you an herbal bath," he said. "For the soreness. And to ensure the viability of the conception."

"You think I'm already with child? From just the one time?"

Jian's fingers spread across her stomach. "I felt the energy move through you. I'm certain the Goddess has blessed this union."

Chanyn felt her world caving in from all sides.

On the one hand, she'd achieved the primary goal of tonight's activities. She was likely pregnant.

On the other hand, she would have to give up the man she loved. She knew this was part of the deal, coming into this room. She just hadn't expected it to be over so soon.

Looking into Jian's face, she saw loss written in his strong jawline.

"Come." He scooped her up into his embrace, holding her with a gentle firmness against his chest.

He carried her to the bathroom, where sweet smelling aromas clouded the air. Jian knelt down to the tub with her in his arms, but Chanyn clung to his neck.

"How long?" she demanded. "How long before you go?"

"The morning." Jian held her eyes. "The water will help to heal any wounds."

He lowered her into the cool water, never taking his eyes off her. The water felt amazing to her skin, to her sore muscles. Jian took a sponge and dipped it into the water, running it down her bare breasts. He bowed over his work with focused attention, each drop he squeezed, a benediction, each movement, a declaration of his love.

All her life, for nearly twenty-one years, Chanyn had been touch-starved. Her mother had no warm embrace, no kind words, no care for her. In the past week Chanyn had made two, possibly three friends. She'd had her hand held. She'd been hugged. She'd been kissed. She'd felt love.

For a moment, she closed her eyes and soaked it all in, overwhelmed by the amount of it.

When Jian's hand stilled, she opened her eyes. His face, usually so neutral, mirrored the awe she felt.

"I used to dream of you," Chanyn said. "All my life, I dreamed that a man would love and care for me. I wanted it so badly. For the last ten years, I dreamed so hard. And here you are. I should be sad, and I am. Sad that I can't keep you."

Water pooled at the edges of Jian's eyes. He shut them tightly, but a solitary tear escaped. "I am sorry."

"Don't be." Chanyn wiped the tear away. "Just because we won't get to see each other anymore, doesn't mean the love stops. Right?"

The liquid brimming at the corners of Jian's eyes filled with want. He reached for her once more. His robes got drenched as he brought her out of the water. He carried her back to the bed, along with a towel. Slowly and methodically, he cleansed each droplet.

It wasn't sexual. It was reverent. When she was dry, Chanyn felt reborn. Jian climbed onto the bed beside her and enfolded her in his arms.

"When I leave in the morning," he whispered. "I'll leave you a gift."

"A gift?"

"Yes," he answered but said nothing further.

Chanyn held him tightly to her. In the morning she would be staying here with her new husbands and growing child. He would return to the temple to continue his work.

His work.

Jealousy reared. "You'll be returning to the temple?"

"Yes," he answered. "There is much work to be done."

Chanyn stiffened in his arms. "Right. Your work."

Goddess, what if she saw him out with another woman? What if he serviced her cousin Merlyn?

Jian reached a hand under her chin and tilted it up. He read her face like reading a book.

"When I return to the temple, I'll be taking vow."

"A vow?"

"Of celibacy."

Chanyn's eyes widened.

"When a hound takes the vow of celibacy, he no longer leaves the temple walls. I won't do the carnal work of a hound any longer. Hounds need compassion to minister to bonded mates. Compassion to see the needs and desires of all sides in the bond. Compassion comes from the heart.

"For so many years my heart was wounded. I never treated the wound and it festered, leaving behind an ugly scar that left me closed, closed to see the needs and desires of others. Until you. You've healed me, cleansed me. I am a man reborn because of you. You've healed my wounded heart. Your mates have restored my sense of compassion. But I can no longer do my duty."

Jian tucked Chanyn's head against his chest and wrapped the rest of his body around hers.

"I can no longer do my duty," he repeated, "because in the morning when I leave, I'm leaving my heart here with you."

CHAPTER EIGHT

"BY THE GODDESS, YOU'RE RIGHT."

Khial's face tightened, along with his fists, as he narrowed his eyes at the Physic who gaped at the second set of test results. His eyes went from the Physic to Chanyn, who sat stiffly on the examination cot. Chanyn wasn't paying the Physic much mind. Her gaze, trained out the window, focused on the domes of the Temple of the Pleasure Hounds which were off in the distance. The full domes, pointing up to the sky towards the Goddess, abreasted the view of the one story fertility clinic.

"You have been bonded less than a week." It wasn't a question, so neither Khial nor Chanyn answered the Physic whose attention was still trained on the results on the tablet screen.

The past few days, Chanyn had been sad. She put on a strong front whenever she came to visit Dain in his sick bed. She read to him, brought him plants and flowers from his mother's garden, lost gracefully at the board games Khial could tell she understood better than she let on.

When Dain slept and she and Khial were left alone together, her smile would fall away. Khial allowed her her sadness. He'd sit with her quietly; take meals with her side by side in a companionable silence neither of them felt the need to fill.

"Pregnant after one coupling. And a girl too."

They had waited the requisite three days it took for gestational chemicals to make themselves known. It was standard to run a gender test with the pregnancy test. The test was strong enough to detect some type of protein present in male offspring. The Physic ran the test twice in search of this protein, though she called it a plague. Chanyn was plague free, which meant that she carried a girl in her womb.

The Physic eyed Khial accusingly. "How did you accomplish this?"

Khial scowled at her, but the menacing look bounced off the older woman.

"We used a Pleasure Hound," Chanyn answered.

The Physic turned to Chanyn. "A monk?"

"Yes, Aunt Angyla."

Khial squinted at Lady Angyla, trying to find the resemblance. He saw the same cinnamon brown skin, though Lady Angyla's looked more like rough, tree bark. They both had the same high cheekbones, but where Chanyn's were often held high in defiance, Lady Angyla's were angular and arrogant. In the end, their eyes outlined their true characters. Lady Angyla's eyes were a cold, metallic gold. Chanyn's churned with life, malleable, begging for hands to mold her and her flesh.

"The hound's rituals worked in just one session with my mates," Chanyn said, a hint of pride in her voice.

Lady Angyla quirked an eyebrow. "And you've only been with your mates? No other—"

"We're done here," Khial grasped Chanyn by the hand. She came off the cot without protest, swinging her legs to the floor and her body into his side. Khial marched them out the door and past the gaping Physic.

Long after they were out of the office, out of the building, and nearing the car, Khial noticed he still held Chanyn's hand firmly in his.

"Sorry," he said releasing her hand.

"I didn't mind," she said.

Khial's discomfort must have read on his face because she continued.

"I actually needed a hand. My back hurts a bit."

He opened the car door for her and handed her inside. She continued talking as he drove.

"I was expecting to be sick in the mornings, but not yet. Just this low ache in my back."

"You're only a few days with child."

"With child," she repeated. She placed her palms gently on her flat stomach.

Khial turned the ignition and pulled onto the road. He couldn't believe they'd created another living being. Well, she and Dain created it. The children of bonded mates were claimed equally by both fathers, though most often you could tell where the child's genetics originated with a long glance. Khial and Dain originated from two different ethnicities. It would be clear to whom the child belonged. But it still didn't negate the fact that Khial was going to be a father.

Suddenly, he felt the nausea that Chanyn had avoided. Khial had no good memories of his fathers. When he did think of father figures, he thought of Dain's fathers. He saw their two smiling faces as they looked down at their son. He remembered a large hand beckoning him to join them in a game, another holding out a seat for him at third meal. As the memories of those two males grew stronger in his mind, the nausea in Khial's gut dissipated.

From the corner of his eye, he caught Chanyn's face. Another series of memories came to mind. Chanyn standing over the boar, a fierce protector to men she hadn't even known. Chanyn leaning forward in the front seat of the car next to him with wonder in her eyes. Chanyn caressing Dain's flushed face with care while sitting beside him on his sick bed.

"For what it's worth, I think you'll be a good mother."

She looked up at him, startled.

"You're kind. You're patient. Those things are important to children."

"I can't imagine where I got those traits. Certainly not from my mother."

"Maybe not," Khial scratched the back of his head. "But what our parents did, how they raised us, made us strong enough to weather the trials we've faced in our lives." Khial thought back to Jian's words. The stubborn tree, he stood tall against the storm.

They pulled up to the house. Khial put the car in park. He rested his hands on the steering wheel.

"I thought that if I let you into the bond it would mean I'd failed," he said. "That my love wasn't enough. But you've been a joy to him. You've made him stronger. Thank you."

Chanyn's lips parted, then closed. Finally, she swallowed. "You're welcome."

Khial turned and got out of the car. He opened the passenger door and offered Chanyn his hand once more. They entered the house in silence, walking side by side, hand in hand. When they reached Dain's room, Khial opened the door for her and let her pass first.

Dain sat with his back against the headboard. His broad body looked small, swathed in all the blankets. Dain's face glowed at the sight of the two of them. The glow belying the continued weakening of his heart muscles and the toll it was taking on the rest of his body. He held his palms up in question.

Chanyn nodded.

A wide grin fell over his face. His arms spread wide and Chanyn went into them. Khial hung back, watching the two, his husband and his wife, embracing.

"You haven't asked if it's a girl or a boy," Chanyn chided him.

Dain shrugged. "I don't care as long as this one's healthy."

This one? So Dain was feeling well enough to expect that he'd be making more. Khial had mixed feelings about that. Chanyn's expression was unreadable, but Khial could guess. He doubted she'd planned a repeat performance without the monk.

But she only said, "It's a girl."

Dain's eyes closed in silent prayer, likely thanking the Goddess for this blessing. When he opened his eyes, he pulled Chanyn to him and kissed her forehead.

"You truly are heaven sent," he declared.

She ran a hand down his face. "You are obviously delirious."

Her jib didn't shake Dain's reverence.

Chanyn rose from the bed. "I'll leave you two alone." She began for the door.

When she came near, Khial caught her hand. And then immediately let it go. Shrugging, he said, "You don't have to go."

Chanyn smiled, rubbing his arm. The spot felt warm even after the brief touch passed. "I'm feeling a little tired." She rubbed her back with a slight wince. "I think I'm going to call it a night."

She gave Khial another warm smile.

He tried to raise the corners of his lips but his mouth felt wobbly. He didn't want to embarrass himself so he released his facial muscles and bowed formally. "Sleep well, my lady."

When he straightened, she paused for a moment. But said nothing and continued on.

Khial went farther into the room and picked up his violin. He put bow to string and looked to Dain for a request. He saw the man grinning at him.

"What?" Khial demanded.

"I'm just happy," he said, a peaceful expression crossing his face. "You two will take care of each other."

"Don't get morbid on me."

"You've been an excellent mate to me. You'll be the same for her."

There was silence. Khial had sat in many comfortable silences with Dain over the years. Never needing to fill the void with chatter. They both knew everything about each other. Except one thing.

"What was it like?" Khial's voice was nearly a whisper.

"What?"

"Being inside of her? What was it like?"

Dain's eyes rose and then slowly lowered, turning thoughtful. "It was like touching a star. They say that at the core of the planet, where the Goddess was born, there's a burning star."

Dain closed his eyes for a moment, in memory. When he opened them, they burned into Khial.

"Making love to Chanyn was just like that. For just a moment, I touched the Goddess."

Khial felt himself heating at the prospect. At the memory of Chanyn's pink flesh, his dick jerked involuntarily.

"I do love her, Khi." Dain shook his slowly head. "Not the same as I do you. It's different. But it is love."

Khial waited for the jealousy to come. It didn't. He thought he understood what Dain meant. He saw the different ways Chanyn looked at Dain and the monk. When she looked at Dain it was with adoration, a mutual respect. When she looked at the monk there was a fire in her eyes. It was the same way Khial looked at Dain. The same look Dain returned to him.

"If you let her, she'll love you, too."

Khial thought of the smile she'd given him today, of the comfort and strength he felt holding her hand.

Emotion remained a scary prospect for him. He'd begun to care for Dain's parents. Darlyn would smile warmly at him. Dain's fathers welcomed him in their rough-housing. Khial had begun to feel safe, secure, cocooned. Then, in the next moment, they were taken from him. Taken from Dain. Taken from the world because of the plague that was his mother. He'd never found out what theory or response his mother attempted to test by causing the accident that had taken the lives' of Dain's parents. She'd been carted off to jail by then.

For a while, he'd believed her motive had been revenge. Revenge against a son who testified against her, her insane research, and the deadly experiment that led to her bond mates' deaths. Revenge against the people who'd banded around her son and had given him the courage to speak up. The only reason he and Dain hadn't been in the conveyance with his parents was due to Dain's illness. He'd been feeling weak that day. Khial volunteered to stay home with him while his parents went out.

It had been years since then. His mother had not struck out at him again, but he knew from experience that she was a patient woman. Khial maintained a vigilant watch over the only person he cared for. Dain was weaker, but he was still here. Chanyn proved herself an ally. He would protect her from any harm. He owed her that much. If not his love, maybe his care and protection.

When Khial looked up, Dain was dosing off. He pulled the sheets over his lover. Not yet tired, Khial decided to grab a bite from the kitchens. When he entered the hall, he stopped short.

The first thing he recognized was blood. Blood on her hands. Blood on her dress. Blood on the floor.

"Chanyn!" He rushed to where she slumped on the floor.

CHAPTER NINE

"IT'S VERY COMMON WITH A first pregnancy; especially when you carry a female child."

Chanyn kept her eyes closed tight. The nausea she had been missing the first few days of her pregnancy roiled through her entire body now. Her forearms clasped about her middle over her empty belly.

"There's nothing to do but try again." Aunt Angyla's voice was methodical, without feeling, unless she imagined the smugness. Angyla ticked off items on her handheld, cocking her head to the right and left like a bird.

The movement made Chanyn think of the first time she'd stolen bird eggs from a nest. She'd felt guilty, but her hunger pangs sent the emotion away quickly enough. Now she was the mother whose nest had been robbed.

A cool hand came to rest on Chanyn's shoulder. The hand trembled in uncertainty as it landed. Chanyn wanted to smile up at Merlyn in encouragement of her awkward attempt at comfort. Though Chanyn was empty, everything felt heavy. She could barely lift her head off the pillow, her body curved into a ball around her barren womb. Chanyn marveled that though she and her cousin had grown up in entirely different environments, Chanyn in solitude, Merlyn surrounded, both had little to no experience with affection and physical contact.

Aunt Angyla lifted her head from her tablet and focused on someone off to the side, in the recesses of Chanyn's room. "I'd like to have you tested," she said.

Khial slowly raised his head to her. He'd been focused on Chanyn, worry warring across his face. His hands clenched and unclenched in impotent helplessness. His hands balled into fists now. The look of worry dissolved into a scowl the likes Chanyn had never seen.

"Tested?" he said.

"Yes," Angyla nodded looking the man up and down like a specimen. "You don't expect me to believe this Hound nonsense."

Chanyn's body jerked at the mention of the hounds. Khial's eyes flicked to her.

"Either you or the other one have the genes to produce girls," Angyla continued. "I'm beginning a trial to harvest male spermatoza and inseminate breeding women. It's a technique from the twentieth century, if you can believe those barbarians did something so forward thinking and civilized. All the records and research were lost in the Great Destruction, but Merlyn, here, is working on a way to isolate the genetic materials that determine the female code."

Merlyn looked down, pride and guilt at odds on her face.

"Soon, there will be no need for copulation," Angyla continued. "Eventually there will be no need for men at all."

Aunt Angyla continued to tap on her tablet, unaware of the three sets of eyes that gaped at her.

"I'll expect you in tomorrow, then."

It was a command, as though Khial were one of her manservants.

Chanyn waited for the blow up, but Khial didn't even bristle. His face was entirely unexpressive.

"Tomorrow's no good for me," he said evenly.

"When, then?" Aunt Angyla looked up, her annoyance plain that her schedule of male eradication would not be met on her timetable.

"Let's see," Khial tapped his lower lip. "I'm free on the fifth of never."

Angyla frowned as she searched for the offered date on her tablet. Finally, she looked up. And blanched. Khial's face was thunderous.

"Out," he ordered quietly, but the sound resonated.

Aunt Angyla swallowed. And then squared her shoulders. "So, you are your mother's child, after all."

"Would you like to stay and find out?"

Angyla made for the door. "Come along, Merlyn. We don't cavort with this kind."

Merlyn gave Chanyn's shoulder a squeeze. "I'll come by later in the week," she whispered. Then she paused and looked up at Khial. "If that's all right?"

Khial looked her over, and then nodded once.

Merlyn rose and followed her mother out, giving Khial a wide berth as she did so.

Khial looked over at Chanyn. He studied her prone form, indecision on his face. Then he left without a word.

Chanyn closed her eyes. She'd never felt so alone in all her life. Her ache was deep. She hadn't even realized she'd wanted the baby so much, until it was gone. She'd done it for Dain, to help him preserve his legacy. Now, all was lost. Dain's health wasn't improving. The tentative camaraderie with Khial was over, as told by his quick departure a moment ago. After Dain went to the Goddess, Khial would have no responsibility towards her, now that the baby was gone.

A wave of pain went through Chanyn as her body continued to purge the life that had barely begun within her. When that ache went dull, another rose to take its place. This time in her heart.

Jian had said he'd leave his heart behind, but right now, all she wanted was his arms around her, his body behind her. Holding her tight, telling her that he had her. That he would take care of it all. That she need only lie back and relax.

The sweetest sound brought Chanyn's eyes open.

Khial sat before her, strumming a beautiful tune on his violin. She hadn't even heard him return. His eyes were closed as he played. Chanyn stared, fascinated, at the array of emotions that crossed his unguarded face as he played for her.

It was like looking through a portal in time. The notes he played told her the story of his life. She saw a young and hopeful boy. A young man full of sadness. A grown man full of guarded compassion. When the song finished, he opened his eyes staring directly into hers. She felt she knew him, entirely, through that song. He didn't smile. His face held that guarded mask once more.

"Rest, my lady. We will take care of you."

He put his bow to string once more and began to play.

Time passed without synchronicity. Chanyn would awaken to Rianald urging her to eat. Another time to Brent and Tem washing her limbs with warm scented water, cooing over her. But most often, she woke to Khial playing. His face unguarded, telling more secrets.

This morning Chanyn woke up entirely alone. Her belly full, her body clean, her spirit light. She sat up, then stood up, and left her room. She found her way down the hall to Dain's room. The door was ajar. She poked her head in and saw him sitting up and reading. He looked duplicitously well. His gold mane shone dull around sallow skin. The muscles of his forearm strained as he held a tablet before his face.

"Dain?"

He instantly dropped the book, startled at her voice. A wide grin broke over his face, crinkling the dark bags under his eyes.

Chanyn came in and closed the door behind her.

"You're looking well," he smiled at her.

"So, are you." She lied and climbed onto the bed.

He immediately grasped her hands, eyes scanning her for wounds. Not of the external variety. He looked her over like he did after her first night with Jian, looking for signs of damage. He looked her over like he did after she fled her family's compound, looking for signs of distress.

Chanyn couldn't hide her pain. Her chin began to wobble. Dain brought her into his arms.

"I'm so sorry, Dain."

He made shushing noises as he rubbed her back.

"You're leaving all you hold dear in my hands and I couldn't even hold on to..."

He pulled her away from him. "I'm supposed to be dead," he said. "Did you know that?"

Chanyn swallowed. Dain was the only one who spoke of his death. Chanyn, Khial and the manservants all avoided the subject by an unspoken agreement.

"I was supposed to have died at birth," Dain ticked the timeframes on his fingers. "Before adolescence. As a teenager. But this time, right now, this was supposed to be it. Last month I was out of miracles. And then I met you. You've kept me here, Chanyn. I brought you here because I thought you were an angel. I asked you to bond with me because I thought you could save the man I love. When I was inside of you, I touched the Goddess. She showed me. She showed me our daughter. She showed me you and Khial raising her together. And She was pleased. I was afraid to die, before. I'm not anymore. It's hard to be fearful when you know you've pleased the Goddess and that you have Her blessings."

Chanyn looked into his smiling face. He had that far off look her mother got during the end of her life, before she went to the Goddess. She knew then that Dain would be leaving soon. There wasn't much time left, but suddenly it all became clear.

Chanyn got off the bed. She reached under her dress and slide off her undergarments.

Dain's eyes widened. "What are you doing?"

Chanyn hitched her skirts and climbed back on the bed, her legs astride Dain's. "What the Goddess foretold."

She reached down below the sheets and found the drawstring of Dain's pants. His eyes were wide, but he let her pull his flesh free. When she pulled him out, he was cool and limp. With a few strokes, he became hot, hard, throbbing.

Chanyn aimed him at her core. She lowered herself slowly, remembering Jian's coaching. Dain was panting before she had him fully seated. His teeth grit in concentration. His hands came to grip her hips. Chanyn began to move slowly. Her eyes never leaving Dain's.

She looked at this man. The first person ever to smile at her. The first person ever to care about her, to check after her well-being. The first person she ever loved.

Chanyn pulled Dain into an embrace as she rode him. They held each other tightly. They held on for dear life. When Dain climaxed a moment later, Chanyn felt it. She felt the presence of energy course through her. She felt it fill her heart.

"Ashe."

CHAPTER TEN

KHIAL STOOD IN THE DOORWAY of his bedroom and waited for the jealousy to consume him. In his bed lay the love of his life curled around his wife. Dain's head rested against Chanyn's heart. His flaccid penis exposed, above the sheets.

Chanyn lay awake, starring off into space. Her hand rubbed circles at the base of Dain's neck. She must have felt Khial's presence because she turned to him. Her hand stilled.

Slowly she extricated herself from Dain. As she rose from the bed, she covered his mid-section. She straightened and made her way to Khial. Once there, she stopped and stood before him, back straight, hands folded in front of her, as though she were waiting for a scolding.

Something churned in his stomach. It rose to his chest, burning away the last bits of buffer around his heart. When the sensation reached his throat, it burst forth as a bark of laughter.

This woke up Dain.

"What's the matter?" Dain asked, his voice croaky with exhaustion.

Khial looked at his weary lover as he struggled from deep sleep to alertness. He returned his gaze to Chanyn. She looked different. Khial couldn't quite put his finger on it, but there was an inner glow, like the halo seen in depictions of the Goddess.

"Nothing," Khial addressed the answer of Dain's question to Chanyn. "Absolutely nothing."

Khial bowed his head to Chanyn.

Chanyn put a hand under his chin. She lifted his head to meet hers. Reaching up on her tiptoes, she planted a small kiss at the side of his mouth.

Khial barely stopped himself from jerking. Not away from her, into her. The feel of her lips was warm, like a shock of lightening. When she pulled away from him, sadness tarnished the gold in her eyes. She looked over her shoulder at Dain and then back at Khial.

"I'll leave you two alone," Chanyn said. She walked out of the room and closed the door behind her.

Khial stood frozen in the center of the room. This place that had been his haven for years. He'd sneak into this room and curl up behind the golden warmth of Dain. Dain was always warm and vibrant, even when caught in the grip of his illness. He was a sun that refused to set. Tonight the room was cold.

Khial looked at Dain who, instead of coming fully alert, had lowered himself to the bed once more. His eyes looked faraway. He could feel Dain leaving. Khial climbed onto the bed and took Dain's hand in his own.

"It's my fault," Khial blurted.

Dain blinked. His foggy gaze focusing on Khial. "What's your fault, my love?"

"Your family's death. It was my mother."

"Khi, what are you talking about?"

"My mother. She caused the crash that killed your parents."

Dain looked at him like a child. "You can't believe that. She was in prison. It was an accident."

Khial shook his head. There were no such things as accidents or coincidences where his mother was concerned. "I've spent all these years trying to make up for it. I've dedicated my life to you, for her crimes."

"Are you trying to tell me you never loved me? That you were only with me out of obligation?"

Khial looked at Dain horrified, but he could tell the other man didn't believe the words he'd spoken.

"Khial, you have filled my life with more happiness and love than any being deserves. My parents saw it, and thanked the Goddess every day for you. Chanyn sees it, too. It's why she agreed to come into the bond. Take care of her when I'm gone. Her and the baby."

Dain had gone delirious. "There is no baby, Dain."

Dain only smiled. He was struggling now to keep his eyes open.

Khial panicked. "Dain! Wait! I love you. I love you, damn it!"

Dain focused once more on Khial, a burst of sunshine before an eclipse. "You think I didn't know that. I knew you did from the first moment you looked at me. I knew I loved you before I walked into the door of the music room. I thought, only the most beautiful human being could make those beautiful sounds. And I was right." Dain smiled and closed his eyes.

"Dain, no. Please don't leave me."

"I'm not leaving. I'll never leave you. I'm going to the Goddess, but I'm leaving my heart. You'll share it with them, won't you Khi?"

Khial would agree to anything to keep Dain's eyes open. "Yes, Dain. I'll share it."

Dain opened his eyes once more. They were so full of love. Khial held that look. He held it for as long as he could. He held it until the light went out of Dain's eyes. And in the end, it was by Khial's hand that Dain's lifeless eyes were closed.

CHAPTER ELEVEN

JIAN WATCHED THE CONTRACTORS DEPART through the front doors of the temple. The new roof was complete, along with many other repairs that had been neglected for the past few years. Jian watched from the doorway as the men piled their tools into the back of their conveyance and then climbed into the front. One man turned back and shouted something.

Jian pointed to his ear, trying to indicate that he couldn't hear the man.

The contractor beckoned Jian forward.

Standing at the edge of the threshold, Jian shook his head. His lips pressed together in a grimace.

The contractor frowned as he hefted himself out of the conveyance and came trudging back to the doorway.

"My apologies," said Jian. "I am bound to the temple. I may not cross the threshold."

The man's face straightened in understanding, but then frowned again. How could he understand a man being confined without bars or restraints? This confinement was of Jian's own choosing. The vow of celibacy came with total dedication to the temple and the Goddess.

The contractor reminded Jian of the necessary follow up service dates and then took his leave once more. Jian watched the man go. The car went in the direction of Lord Dain's manse. Jian allowed himself one more second in the cool open air, and then he retreated into the sanctuary.

The exterior of the temple received a fresh coat of paint, but when Jian looked closely, he still saw the cracks and crumbling in the brick. The roof was repaired, but Jian still needed to sort out the refuse above his head in the attic. As the building received work on its exterior structure, there was much work to be done for the inner workings to return to their former glory.

Jian escaped into the heart of the temple, the Sanctuary, where all the monks met daily to show their devotion to the Goddess. The room was empty now, at midday. Jian stood for a moment in the silence.

Elder Gerry appeared beside Jian. "We have two more new recruits today, my brother."

Four young males had been brought to the temple by families. Proof that word of Jian's success with Lady Chanyn had spread.

"You've done it, my boy." Elder Gerry glowed with pride.

It took everything Jian had to muster the briefest of smiles.

"I think it was a wise decision to take the vow," the elder man continued. "Now you can put all of your heart into training the next generation of hounds."

All of his heart? Jian looked around at the empty Sanctuary. He couldn't tell the elder man that he'd left his prized teaching tool with the woman responsible for his success. Jian urged away the thought of Chanyn's smile, her body, the feel of her lips on his. He did not berate himself for the thoughts, only the timing.

Tonight, he promised himself.

Like all nights. He would lie in his bed and remember every moment he'd spent with her, in detail. He gave another gentle shove to the memories.

Tonight, he promised.

"Speaking of the next generation," Elder Gerry turned and faced Jian, his excited face now somber. "I received a note. Your patron, Lord Dain, has returned to the Goddess."

Jian's breath ceased. He saw Lord Dain in his mind's eye. The picture of golden health. He hadn't fully believed Lord Dain when he said he was dying.

"We will light a candle in his memory," said Elder Gerry and then he moved on.

Sadness fell on Jian. He'd known Lord Dain a short time, but the thoughtful, generous, kind man left a strong imprint on Jian. He was a model of compassion. Had Lord Dain not been a first son, he would have made an excellent hound. Lord Khial would be devastated at the loss of his mate. So would—

"Elder Gerry."

They had moved to the common area of the temple. Bowed heads rose and turned to face Jian. He had spoken at a normal volume. Normal was too loud in the quiet temple.

Jian took large steps, in lieu of running, to catch up with his mentor. "Elder Gerry," he said, at a more agreeable volume. "Was there any news of the lady?"

Elder Gerry's eyes went sad as he nodded his head once more. Jian's gut clenched, alerting him before words passed Elder Gerry's lips that something was amiss.

Elder Gerry put his hand on Jian's shoulder. The weight of his hand heavy. "The lady lost the child."

Ice ran down Jian's back. "Why didn't you tell me?"

Elder Gerry's eyes widened in surprise. Jian's voice had risen to a shout.

"It was during the time you took your vows and were in seclusion."

Jian felt hollowed out.

"Where are you going," Elder Gerry called after him.

Jian hadn't realized his feet started moving. He headed back to the front door of the temple. The life-giving sun sat low on the horizon. Jian could see it's decent into darkness. His foot bumped a ceremonial rug as he approached the threshold. With each step his heart pounded to life in his ears. If he made a step over that threshold, he'd break his vows. He might never be allowed to return to his home.

His feet never slowed as they stepped over the threshold and onto fresh grass.

He ran the distance to Lord Dain's, now Lady Chanyn's, home. Heart pounding louder with every step closer to her.

When he reached the door the manservant, Rianald, didn't look surprised to see him. He looked relieved.

"She's in her room," he said and closed the door behind Jian.

Jian took the steps two at a time. Arriving at her door, he paused. It was silent inside. He raised his hand and knocked.

No response.

He knocked once more.

Still no response.

He opened the door.

She lay in the bed, staring off into space, her hand cradling her belly. Jian noticed an untouched tray of food on a stand near her bed. He supposed he wasn't her first visitor, and that's why she didn't startle at his entry.

He went to the bed and sat down. That caught her attention.

She blinked up at him. Once, then twice before her face broke into recognition.

"Hi," she said.

"Hello," his voice croaked.

"You're here."

"I am," he agreed.

She reached for his hand. Once it was within her grasp, she held it tightly to her heart, and closed her eyes once more.

Jian ran his free hand up the side of her face. His memory had done him a great justice. He'd remembered the angles of her jaw, the softness of her cheeks, the arch of her brows exactly, perfectly.

"I'm so sorry, my love." Jian stretched his body alongside hers and brought her into his arms.

"Don't be," she sighed. "He..." She squeezed her eyes shut. When she opened them, Jian saw a sad sort of joy. "He was truly blessed. His entire life, everything and everyone he touched. I will miss him every day for the rest of my life. But I will also be thankful for every day of his life that I got to share."

Jian tucked Chanyn's head into his chest and rubbed her back.

"I thought you took your vows?" she said.

"I did."

"But you said you couldn't leave again, after you took the vows."

"I couldn't ignore my heart breaking." He placed his hand over the space on her chest. She gripped it as though it were a lifeline.

He leaned down to kiss her, but at the last second, she pushed against his chest. A shudder went through her body. She clasped her hand over her mouth, leaped out of the bed, and dashed into the bathroom.

Jian heard the sounds of purging. He rushed to her side. Kneeling on the tiled floor, he held her hair. When she finished, he grabbed a towel and cleaned her up.

Then he studied her. "They told me you'd..."

"I did lose the first child."

"First?"

Chanyn nodded. "Then we tried again."

An irrational sweep of jealousy passed through Jian that Chanyn had engaged in love making without him present.

"I felt her, Jian," Chanyn's eyes were bright. "The Goddess. I felt her move through me to create this life inside me." She cradled her belly, her eyes filling with tears. "She gave us this life, and then she took Dain."

Jian looked down at Chanyn's belly. There was no bump through the fabric of her dress. The child in question couldn't be more than a few days old, but Jian didn't doubt the baby's existence.

He finished cleaning Chanyn up. Then he gathered her in his arms and carried her back to the bed. He bent over and laid her down gently. When he went to straighten, she clung to him.

"Stay," she pleaded.

When Jian left the temple nearly a half hour ago, he'd given no thought to where he would end up after he made certain Chanyn was well. Breaking vows was taken seriously, and Jian might very well not be invited back into the only home he ever knew. But he couldn't stay in the home of a bonded lady either.

"Where's your mate? Where's Lord Khial?"

Anguish returned to Chanyn's face. "I don't know," she said.

The man was grieved. He was likely out assuaging his grief. "I'll stay until he returns." Then Jian would have to figure out what to do with his life.

"That might be a long time," Chanyn said. "He hasn't been home in days. Not since Dain..."

Jian played Chanyn's words over again in his head. They couldn't be right. The man wouldn't abandon his pregnant wife. It was simply unheard of.

Jian's own plight would have to wait. There was only one thing for him to do. "I'll find him for you."

PART THREE

CHAPTER ONE

THE MOON PULLED ANCHOR AND sailed high into the heavens while the sun released its hold on the horizon and sank. Somewhere between the two celestial bodies, Khial drifted. He'd wandered around for days. Two days? Three, maybe? Time scattered around him, stretched and distorted like the pieces of a popped balloon.

Looking up at the moon left Khial light-headed. The white orb filled the sky, its body swollen, its seams set to burst. Memories of old swirled in Khial's head, sending him back to boyhood.

As a boy, to escape the incessant mind games played by his parents during mealtimes, one day Khial ventured out into the street market. Khial's first trip to the market was also his last. He clutched his throat, watching a man fry gray meat in a grease-laden pan. His toes curled at the screeching of a three-piece, musical ensemble. He flipped up his collar at the sight of two scrawny, unwashed street boys near his age.

Turning his back on them, Khial spotted a blue orb. The balloon stretched and yearned for the sky, but was tethered to earth by a silver string. Its captor, an old man with gray hair and clear gray eyes, like a reflecting mirror, gazed down at Khial. His gnarled hands twisted oblong balloons into animal shapes.

Khial reached in his pocket and withdrew a piece of copper. In exchange, the old man handed him a contorted balloon in the shape of a lion. Before turning away, Khial cast one final glance at the captive blue balloon. It bobbed and weaved, testing the restraints of the string. And then suddenly, it was yanked down, free.

Khial blinked as the gnarled hand placed the string before him. He reached into his pocket before reaching for the proffered balloon, but the old man shook his head. He released the balloon into Khial's hand, with a wink.

On the way home Khial's hands were full. He cradled the lion in one arm, in the other hand his five fingers wrapped around the silver string, tight. No one had ever given him a gift before.

Khial returned home to the sounds of fists popping jaws. His fathers were fighting over his mother once more. His mother, Lady Danyell, stood at the top of the stairs monitoring her mates' progress.

Early in his young life, Khial believed his mother was the Goddess, Herself. Her skin was as dark as the fertile earth, her hair a fluffy cloud that haloed around her face. The vacancy in her eyes proved his infantile theory wrong.

Lady Danyell held no tablet in her hands to record whatever experiment she'd set into motion. She possessed a photographic memory that catalogued and compartmentalized everything she witnessed, read, or heard. His mother was fascinated with the emotions of jealousy. Not being able to feel the emotion herself, she doubted, its existence and used her husbands to test its variables.

The crash of one of Khial's fathers falling startled him, and his grip relinquished the silver string. His gift sailed up to the high ceilings, far beyond his reach. His face fell. His eyes teared. Before he could correct his mistake, his mother appeared before him.

Danyell's calculating gaze looked from her son's face, to the floating balloon before settling on the contorted material still in Khial's arms.

"Why are you crying." There was no inflection in her voice to indicate that the statement was a question. For Lady Danyell it was a problem, a hypothesis she meant to investigate.

"It's still present," she indicated the floating balloon. "It's simply beyond your reach."

She cocked her head to the side at her statement, turning it over and over again in her clockwork mind. She held her hand out for the contorted balloon that remained in Khial's hand. Khial knew it was fruitless to deny her. He shuttered himself against further loss and handed the balloon over. Without preamble, his mother squeezed the balloon until the air burst from it, rending the elastic into pieces. The stretched and distorted pieces landed on the floor in a quiet crash.

"This one is also still present." She held up the pieces, ticking off the variables. "This one is in your reach. Though its function is now useless."

Danyell tick-tocked her head in the opposite direction, investigating from a different angle. Khial focused on his mother's shoulder, his head high, his teeth grit, his face blank.

"So, why is it that you cry? Is it the loss of function or the loss of proximity?"

Khial didn't answer. They stood there for a long, silent moment. Until another crash broke her contemplation. Lady Danyell tick-tocked her head in the direction of her mates and followed in the wake of their debris.

Khial ran out of the house and hid in the woods. That day he stayed in his hiding spot until it grew dark.

It was dark out now. Khial didn't know where he was, nor how he'd gotten here. The last thing he remembered was the light go out of Dain's eyes and the silence that crashed around him. Dain's body remained present, perfectly intact, but empty and beyond Khial's reach.

Khial glanced up at his surroundings. He was far from the clean, wealthy side of town where women lived. He was beyond the market where the rich and working class bartered. The three story high-rises crunched together on dirt patches of land signaled that Khial's wanderings had brought him to the end of genteel civilization. Only male bodies, young, mature, and elderly, littered these streets. The discarded thirds and enterprising second sons ruled these outskirts. Many hungry, calculating, desperate eyes landed on Khial like a swarm of flies on a carcass. What little self-preservation he had left told him he needed to get off the streets if he wanted to make it to morning.

Khial stood still.

He'd drifted for days in an effort to untether himself from this world. Perhaps if he stood still long enough, someone would come by and pop him off. The idea held merit, but Khial's legs wobbled. Perhaps in the morning, he would stand firm in the middle of the streets and wait for oblivion. For now, Khial ducked into a boarding establishment.

Though the Sisterhood had no care for or reach into the outskirts, their charity provided a number of free shelters where males could get a cot and a warm meal for the night. Looking around the interior of one such establishment, Khial realized he'd never seen so much squalor. He could make out each grimy fingerprint on the wall. Cakes of dirt decorated the corners of the room. Filth stained the cot mattresses, a chorus of rusty springs sang lullabies. The men all smelled. Khial took one look in the showers and turned the other way.

It baffled him. He'd always thought women held high standards for the shelters of the city's discarded boys. He'd been told the discards lived in clean homes and received three square meals a day. His stomach protested as it tried to digest the stale bread, bruised vegetables, and questionable meat.

He couldn't complain too much. In truth he'd taken a step down when he came to live with Dain and his family. Dain's family home had been a small cottage compared to the splendor that was his mother's royal estates. Khial never felt a sense of belonging amidst the jeweled fixtures, the priceless art, and the antique furnishings of his status. He walked away from all of that to be with the boy he loved and his infamous parents.

Color vibrated from every corner of Dain's home. Nothing in glass, nothing broken. Shouts of joy rang out morning, noon, and night. His family gave gifts frequently, never taking them back to measure a child's response or condition a behavior.

Khial would often sit on the sidelines and watch Dain's fathers play with him. Watch the affection they had for each other and their wife. Watch them hug and kiss. They offered the same affection to Khial, but soon realized that it was difficult for him to receive. Khial remained wary of grown men and women. The only person whose embrace felt right was Dain's.

There was an ancient saying: Home is Where the Heart is. Whenever Khial laid his head at Dain's heart he felt peace, he felt safe, he felt home.

And now his home was gone.

The rusty bed groaned as Khial slumped down onto it. His shoulders caved in, curling around his chest. He'd chosen a cot in the corner, the farthest away from the others. As the night settled, the room began to fill with bodies. They were a haze to Khial, who couldn't see much farther than his hands. He clenched and unclenched his left hand. At turns trying to dull the ache in his chest. At other points trying to get feeling once more in his limbs.

"Did you hear me, turd? I said, that's my bed!"

Khial looked up slowly. The thick body of a man came into focus. Slightly less filthy than the others, this man looked young, younger than Khial.

The man surveyed Khial from head to toe and then back again, as though Khial's two halves didn't quite fit. Khial knew he must look filthy from wearing the same clothes for days. He hadn't taken anything with him when he left the house. When he'd felt Dain's spirit leave his body, Khial felt himself become untethered to this world. What need did a balloon have of clothing? Cloth was like string and Khial wanted to be free.

The man peered down at Khial, his menacing mug changing slowly to something else. "If you're comfortable there, I would consider letting you share with me."

"I beg your pardon?" Khial tilted his head to the side, his foggy brain grasped for comprehension.

The man grinned. "Oh, I'll make you beg."

In a flash, the grin turned to a leer. A hand reached out and cuffed Khial at his ear. For a moment, Khial stared at that meaty palm. His chin pressed into the soft flesh left by the space between the man's thumb and forefinger. Khial realized with amusement that he was being manhandled. Literally.

A chuckle broke the surface of Khial's fogged brain and then his world turned off kilter as the meaty fist gave him a powerful shake.

"You think yourself funny, you little pansy?"

Khial met the man's eyes and startled. His head ticktocked the other way, and then swung back again as he grasped for focus. The man's eyes were green, like Dain's. Only there was no mischievous light in the man's eyes. Khial glanced behind the man to see a crowd had gathered. They stood at a distance, no one willing to lend their own hand.

"It's clear you don't belong here, pansy. But since you stopped by I'll make you mine for the night. What you show me under the sheets will tell me what I do with you in the morning."

Khial's head straightened. He faced the vile man head on. Of all the insults hurled at him, the man's claim of ownership brought Khial out of his stupor. The only man who could lay that claim was gone. Khial clenched his hands to get feeling in them. Clenched them once more and then swung his arm.

The element of surprise must have been on his side. The man released him and stumbled back. Both he and Khial stood there in shock. The man must not have thought it in Khial. Khial could not have blamed him. Though he'd watched his fathers do it time and again to each other, he'd never hit another human being before.

It felt good. Getting that aggression out of him. For half of his life people had looked at him as though violence would burst from his person at any moment. That he would unleash the monster his mother had created. Though he'd never committed a single act of violence in his entire life, people in polite society would cringe as he walked by. Khial would often cringe as he caught sight of himself in the mirror.

When he looked again at the man on the floor, bile rose in Khial's throat. His meal threatened to encore. Gone was the elation at releasing the aggression. Khial reached out his hand towards the man. He was met with a swift kick to the face.

Khial fell back sideways onto the bed. By the time he sat up, the man had regained his feet, and he didn't stand alone. Two other men stood beside him. The man charged towards Khial.

Khial clenched his fists once more, willing the adrenalin, the anger, the aggression to return to him. It didn't.

He unclenched his five fingers, releasing his tie to the world. He envisioned the blue balloon sailing off into the heavens.

Khial closed his eyes and waited for the pop of impact.

Then, he heard it. Pop! But he didn't feel it.

And then another. Pop! Followed by a succession of pops. Khial opened one then another eye. A flurry of robes flashed before him.

The monk moved like Khial played. Fluid, never ceasing the melody. Khial watched the notes form as the monk's feet spun, spread, and came back together. His arms spread wide, striking out but wrapping around a neck instead of punching. His hands came together cupping an incoming fist and twisting it to its limit without snapping the joint.

When the monk had finished, the three men lay in heaps on the floor. Incapacitated and bruised, but not bloody. The fight had been elegant, no brute force used.

"Out! Out!" The shelter manager bellowed from above.

Jian looked up at the man. The fight seeped out of his rigid shoulders, an inscrutable looked settled on his handsome face. It may have been shame. That would make sense. The man was a monk. Didn't monks swear never to harm?

Jian turned to Khial and motioned for him to precede him. Once outside, Jian looked around, appearing lost for a moment. The moon glowed bright as the sun in the dead of night. The silent streets had emptied of all souls.

"What are you doing here?" Khial asked.

Jian tilted Khial's head back and surveyed his bruise. "I came for you."

The cradle of Jian's warm palm threatened to tether Khial once more to the earth. But then Jian's harsh tone snapped the string.

"Those places are dangerous," the monk admonished. He placed both hands on Khial's shoulders and gave him a shake. "They're no place for a lord."

Khial could only focus on the warm feel at his shoulders. Moments ago, they had been numb, but he could still clearly feel where each of the monk's fingers touched him, pulling him down to the ground.

Khial shook the sensation off. "I'm not lord of anything."

"Your birthright made you a lord."

"My birthright?" Khial laughed. "My birthright is one of insanity and murder."

The monk shook his head. "We write our own pasts, Lord Khial."

Khial ignored that. "I didn't know monks could fight."

Jian put them both in motion towards the inner city. "The great thinker, Buddha, had a constant adversary: Mara. After a time, Buddha saw Mara lying in wait to trap him. Buddha did not run from his adversary. Buddha told Mara, I see you. Can you guess what he did next?"

"Buddha sucker punched Mara in the face?"

Jian made an amused sound in his throat. "No," he said.

He eyed Khial as his grade school teacher had when he'd tried to teach him something. Khial's grade school teacher knew he was smart. Knew that Khial listened, but refused to allow the lesson to penetrate.

"The Buddha said to Mara, 'Come have tea.' Buddha wanted to understand his adversary, for only then could he truly defeat him."

"I didn't see you ask any of those thugs for tea," Khial challenged.

Jian's laugh was humorless this time. "No, I understand men like that. I was a street turd before I was a monk."

Jian reached out and put a hand on Khial's shoulder. Again, the heat from his fingers penetrated through the fog of Khial's brain.

"I am sorry for your loss, my lord. I know you must be grieving, but your family needs you."

"I don't have a family."

"You have a wife and a child."

Khial's chin dropped to his chest. He hadn't thought of Chanyn in the last three days. He'd assumed she would not care to keep the bond with him, especially after losing both the baby and Dain. But the monk had said wife and child.

Khial thought back to the day of Dain's death. They had been together, Dain and Chanyn. Dain had said he felt the Goddess, that she'd blessed the union. She'd blessed Dain and then took him away, out of Khial's reach, leaving an empty vessel behind.

"Dain was my home and now he's gone."

"Dain is at your home," Jian said.

Khial's breath hitched, his eyes widened. Jian rested his hand once more on Khial's shoulder. The compassionate expression on the monk's face deflated any false hope that seeped into Khial's chest.

"Dain lives inside your wife's womb. That child is a part of him. As much as Chanyn cared for Dain, she didn't know him as you did. That child will need to know its father, both fathers. That child will need you, Lord Khial."

Khial looked up into the night's sky. The stars twinkled at him, beckoning him to sail away.

Jian began walking once more, back to civilization. Behind him, Khial followed. His feet heavy with each step on the earth, each strike of his heel a new tether.

CHAPTER TWO

"SHE'S LOST THE ONE MATE and the other deserted her. Certainly the property reverts to the family." Dain's uncle, Bil, pawed at an ancient china bowl on the windowsill. His lips curled, barring a sharp grin.

"A male's bloodline does not usurp a woman's rights." Chanyn's Aunt Angyla stood near the fireplace on the other side of the room, away from Bil, looking down her nose at her surroundings and its occupants.

They'd gathered in Dain's office. Chanyn sat on the settee where Dain proposed to her weeks ago. The memory clung to the forefront of her mind, strong and bright.

Bil moved before the window, blocking the morning sun. Angyla crossed in front of the fireplace, the last ember went dark. Chanyn cradled her elbows to her chest, rubbing the goose bumps that rose. Along with the bumps, another memory rose in her mind.

At the age of ten Chanyn woke to find her mother gone. She'd felt sad, but not scared. She understood the workings of the ruins she lived in. She knew how to gather food from the garden and collect water from the rain barrels. She was alone, but she lived relatively the same as she had each day of her life. Not much changed that day, not even when her mother returned the next morning.

Tonight, in a room full of family members, Chanyn felt an, aloneness, unlike before. In the space of a month, she'd met her true love, found a true friend, and earned the trust of an ally. After a lifetime of being alone, for the first time Chanyn felt abandoned.

Bil and Angyla continued to bicker over Dain's property and wealth. Chanyn tuned them out.

A warm hand took Chanyn's. The grasp was awkward.

Merlyn.

She rubbed Chanyn's hand as though she were trying to wipe off a smudge. Her unpracticed smile was lopsided. "Don't worry. Mother won't let him take your wealth. Though it's probable that she will entangle the funds in the family coffers beyond your reach."

"The money doesn't matter to me."

Chanyn's currency had always been love and affection. Dain's friendship alone filled her well, and then he brought her Jian. Chanyn would give every cent of the money, every acre of the property to these people if only she could have Dain and his generous heart back.

Merlyn opened her mouth. Then closed it. She took a breath, leaned into Chanyn and spoke. "Did you love him?" The edges of her eyes bunched when she said the word love, squinting as though peering into the sun.

Chanyn looked into her cousin's curious eyes. Eyes that reminded her of her mother. But unlike her mother's quest for data, there was the growing warmth of compassion at the corner of Merlyn's eyes. Chanyn realized the younger woman asked because she wanted to understand, not catalogue the answer.

Chanyn nodded in response. "I do... did love him." The tense tripped her tongue.

Merlyn leaned in closer, eager. "Could you describe the indications to me? But not viscerally, quantitatively if possible?"

Chanyn tried to find the words to give the feelings measurement, and failed. "I felt a part of something. I felt wanted. I felt..." And there the feelings failed her, so she reached for a fact. "He was my friend."

Merlyn nodded at this last statement, as though she could grasp the fact better than the meaning. Her eyes went dreamy, unfocused, as though she were peering into the past. "I had a friend once."

Chanyn squeezed her cousin's hand. "You have a friend now."

Merlyn startled. Then relaxed under Chanyn's hand. Chanyn gave her cousin another squeeze. And then she gripped her cousin's hand tightly. A wave of nausea threatened. Chanyn took a couple of deep breaths. Merlyn awkwardly patted her back. The rubbing motion wasn't helping, but Chanyn didn't want to dissuade the other woman's infantile steps toward affection. She needed a steady hand right now.

Her stomach convulsed again. Chanyn's hands flew to her womb as though she could protect the novel life in there. Her aunt and Bil continued to argue, their voices grating on Chanyn's nerves as she held her breakfast in, refusing to let go of anything more. Dain had given Chanyn his entire world, and the moment after he left the earth she was barely clinging to what remained.

The nausea relaxed its grip and she stood up. "Quiet!"

All eyes went to her. Chanyn took a deep breath, preparing to speak. Unfortunately, she'd stood up a little too quickly.

Chanyn dashed for the china bowl that Bil coveted and promptly emptied her belly into it.

When she straightened, Bil's eyes were bright. "She's ill." He barely masked the delight.

"No, idiot," said Angyla. "She's pregnant."

"But, she lost the baby," Bil protested.

They all looked to Chanyn for conformation.

"The sudden vomiting so closely after first meal suggests a second pregnancy," Angyla continued. "The sickness happens due to a high level of hormones the body produces to protect the placenta. That indicates this pregnancy will be viable."

Chanyn took another deep breath. She straightened her spine, wiped her mouth, and prepared to speak. But something in the door caught her attention. Actually, it was someone.

Jian.

He stood in his robes, a bit disheveled as though he hadn't slept or washed in the day he'd been gone.

Chanyn wanted nothing more than to run into his arms and hide while he soothed her.

"Is that a hound?" Aunt Angyla sneered. "You let hounds into your house?"

Chanyn saw Jian's eyes lower, his head bow. She was about to tell her aunt off when she caught something behind Jian. Or rather someone.

Chanyn did take off running then. She moved past Bil as he pocketed a smaller piece of china, past her aunt who pressed herself into the far corner, past Jian whose arms opened for her. Chanyn ran straight up to Khial and wrapped her arms around his neck. She could tell this startled him, because for a moment he stiffened. Then tentatively, slowly, his arms came about her. Chanyn couldn't stop herself. She began to weep. As her body began to shake, Khial's grip on her firmed.

"Out," she heard him say. "All of you. Out."

He spoke quietly, but his voice resonated, brooking no argument.

From her place buried in his neck, Chanyn heard the shuffling of feet passing her by.

"Lady Merlyn," she heard Khial say. "You're welcome to return whenever it pleases you."

Chanyn couldn't see her cousin's response, but felt certain she would be seeing Merlyn sometime soon.

Chanyn didn't know how long she stayed wrapped up in Khial. She kept her focus on his strong arms, the soft cushion between his neck and shoulder, the strong beat of his heart. He was the first to break the silence.

"I'm sorry," he said.

Finally, Chanyn broke away from him. They were alone, just the two of them.

"Promise me—" Chanyn had to stop, clear her throat and try again. "Promise me you won't leave me again." It took courage to beg. Chanyn had no fear facing down a wild animal, but a pair of greedy humans proved a far different story. She never wanted to face the beasts on her own again.

Khial hesitated.

Chanyn went on. "I know I'm not him. I'll never be what he was to you. But you and I are the only two people who loved him. And now his child grows inside me. I can't do this alone. I mean, I could, but I don't want to. I don't want this child to grow up without its father, like I did. I want it to have a loving home, like Dain did. I don't know what that looks like. You do."

Khial looked at her, helpless. "I always felt like a guest here."

She clasped his hands in her own. It wasn't like in the romance novels where the lady's hands were dainty and the man had large paws. Both Chanyn and Khial had strong, callused, capable hands. "We could do it together. We don't have to be true bonded mates in the physical sense if you don't wish it. But we could be the parents we never had."

Khial looked at her doubtfully, but Chanyn could see a slight flicker in his eyes. "You'd trust me with a child?"

Chanyn frowned. "Why wouldn't I?"

"Don't you know about my parents?"

"I know they made bad decisions and hurt one another. My mother was not an ideal parent either. But we don't have to be them. I trust you. You've always been honest with me. You were distant because you didn't know me and you were trying to protect Dain. But I don't think for a second that you would hurt anyone or anything. For Goddess sake, you could barely handle a boar."

Khial's bark of laughter took them both by surprise. He looked down at her midsection and then into her eyes.

"I don't know what kind of father I'll be," he said. "But I promise I won't leave you again."

Chanyn heaved a sigh of relief. She was hugging him again before she realized he might not like it. But he gave no resistance.

CHAPTER THREE

JIAN KNEW THAT LORD KHIAL'S eviction didn't extend to him, but he left the room nonetheless.

He'd kept a steady hand on the young lord the whole way home. Only moments ago, the man could barely make it up the steps to his home. Ghosts lived in those sky blue eyes. Jian didn't feel an ounce of jealousy, bitterness, or regret when Chanyn ran into Lord Khial's stiff arms. Instead, he wanted to instruct Lord Khial on how to hold her properly. That she liked it when you rested a firm hand at the small of her back. That she'd become entirely pliable if you placed a second hand at the base of her neck.

But Jian held silent. Instruction was no longer his trade. He'd promised the rest of his life to the Goddess, away from her daughters and the men who aimed to please them.

Jian walked down the hall with the same heavy steps that Lord Khial marched up them.

"You're not staying the night?" The manservant, Rianald, materialized before him.

Jian kept his back to the staircase that led to the sleeping quarters. He shook any last desire from his head.

"You have honored this house," Rianald bowed. "You have done well for this family. I'm sure the Lady Darlyn smiles on you alongside her son from their place with the Goddess."

Jian's mouth wouldn't work to respond. He bowed.

He stepped outside the front door of the house into the windless day. A pressure pushed him backwards as he stepped over the threshold. Jian pushed his way on and heard raised voices.

"That girl needs serious guidance!"

At the base of the stairs stood Lady Angyla and her daughter Lady Merlyn.

"Marrying the son of murderers and the son of pornographic actors." Lady Angyla spotted Jian and her face soured even more. "And cavorting with sex workers."

Jian looked away.

A conveyance pulled up to the curb and a manservant hopped out to take Lady Angyla's hand. She glanced back at the house with disgust. "That girl is a lost cause. Come along Merlyn."

But Lady Merlyn hesitated. She turned to Jian and climbed one step.

"You're a..." The lady leaned in and whispered. "A Pleasure Hound?"

Jian wasn't quite sure if he should answer after her mother's admonishment. He bowed his head.

Lady Merlyn climbed two more steps. "Do you happen to know a hound by the name of Jaspir?"

Jian did know that name. "Yes, my lady. I trained with him."

She took the remaining steps until she stood level with Jian. "So, he's still... at the temple?"

"No, my lady. Jaspir did not take the vows. For a Pleasure Hound to take the vows his heart must be free. You cannot serve the Goddess and man. A hound is only the vessel of the Goddess, to be used by her. Jaspir's heart belonged to another."

Lady Merlyn's golden-brown eyes brightened, reminding Jian of Chanyn's. "Because of love?"

"Yes, my lady."

Lady Merlyn's hand rose to her lips, then hovered at her heart.

"Did you know Jaspir?"

Lady Merlyn nodded, her smile brightened her face. Again, Jian saw the family resemblance. "He was my friend." And then a frown dragged one side of her smile down. "But if he's not at the temple, where is he?"

"The last I heard he was working at... The Stallion."

Lady Merlyn's frown deepened, bringing the other side down. By the look on her face, Jian assumed she knew what kind of carnal establishment The Stallion was.

"My lady?" The manservant from the car came forward with his hand outstretched. Lady Merlyn descended the stairs and allowed herself to be put in the car.

Jian stole one more glance at the house. He tucked it tight into his memory, and then walked away.

He strolled slowly, leisurely. The steps he'd taken recently limited him to the confines of the temple. In the last five years, when he found himself outside of the temple, he'd walked with a purpose to get food or supplies. But now he simply walked for the joy of it. Feeling the earth crunch beneath his feet, the strength and the certainty in the firmament of the Goddess who cradled them all.

Jian concentrated on stepping lightly on the earth. Imagining first his skin, then his muscle, and finally the bones of his feet touching the earth lightly. He gave himself over to the exercise fully, allowing the earth to support him. Knowing that with each step toward the temple, he was headed in the right direction. Back to his life's purpose, to be in total service to the Goddess. Behind him, Chanyn remained in good hands. She and Lord Khial would make it together. Jian focused his attention on letting her go, replacing his arms around her waist, his lips on hers with Lord Khial's.

He lost himself in the simple task of walking. One foot in front of the other. Needing to please no one but the Goddess. Needing to think of nothing. Empty. Weightless. An offering that She would find pleasing to fill up with her will.

The walk from Chanyn's home to the temple took thirty minutes at a leisurely pace. Somehow, morning turned to night before Jian returned home. He saw that he had a welcoming party.

Elder Gerry sat in an old bamboo chair just outside the entrance to the temple. His face upturned, gazing at the stars. It was a favorite pastime of the old monk. He'd taught Jian to read the stars. In the night's sky, Jian spied Orion burning bright. Often depicted as a great warrior, Orion's story also told of epic love, sacrifice, and constant pursuit.

The two men returned their gazes to the earth at the same time. Elder Gerry sighed and the peace Jian had cultivated over his walk cracked.

"I never told you why I came to this place," Master Gerry began. "As a second son, I fell in love with my brother's bond mate. She and I were great friends. I knew she preferred me to my brother. So, one day I told her of my feelings. She admitted she felt the same way. We made love. Once. And then she married my elder brother as promised."

He closed his eyes as though shaking the memories from his head. "I couldn't watch them, day in and day out. So I left. I left her and my family behind. I came here and I dedicated myself to the Goddess. Soon, I came to love the Goddess—not more than my lady, but differently. It's not equivalent—what I felt for that girl and what I feel for our deity."

Elder Gerry rocked back in his chair, his face upturned to the stars once more. "She became ill ten years ago, the girl I loved. I had great responsibilities here. If I left the temple, even for a few weeks, it would have put the brothers in a bad way. So I stayed. She died.

"The Goddess is my one true love. Most people love another human being. If they're lucky, that love is returned. Men like us who have not received the love of a mother; we are perfect servants to the Goddess. We can devote our entire selves to her. She is our mother, our friend, and our one true love."

Elder Gerry looked Jian square in the eyes. "If Lady Chanyn called out to you again, would you go?"

Jian didn't have to think about his answer. It was, "Yes." If Chanyn stubbed her toe and called out to him, he'd go to her.

Elder Gerry nodded. "And that is why you cannot cross this threshold to rejoin your brothers. Our mistress is a selfish one. To serve as we do you must give all your heart to Her. We serve all her daughters equally, not one more than another."

Jian stared down at his feet as they took a step back.

"What you feel for your lady is not wrong. Neither is it right. It just is. You will be sorely missed. By me, most of all."

Elder Gerry rose from his chair and came to Jian, halting his backward progression.

Elder Gerry embraced Jian. "Our ancient brother Rumi says that there is a field beyond the ideas of wrongdoings and rightdoings. One day I'll meet you there, my son."

Jian untied his robe and put on the proffered cotton shirt that Elder Gerry held out to him. The material itched his skin. He took the sack of his belongings. Then he walked away from his home.

CHAPTER FOUR

KHIAL CLENCHED AND THEN UNCLENCHED his fist, his shoulder ached from being suspended in midair.

"Dain told me that the garden is so lush because his mother still watches over it," Chanyn said beside him.

"Oh?"

Chanyn's hand perched on Khial's arm. His elbow pointing toward her breasts, as he'd seen bonded males of high society walk with their ladies. Khial felt ridiculous.

"Does it bother you to speak of him?"

Khial clenched the fist of his suspended arm. The bunching muscles caught Chanyn's fingertips in the crook of his elbow.

Chanyn nudged her fingers out of his crook. "I can stop if it bothers you."

"No, no." Khial unclenched his fist, but they automatically clenched again. "Well, yes. It's just too soon right now. But another time. Perhaps."

Chanyn removed her hand entirely from his arm. "Khial, do you mind if we sit down?"

"Of course." Khial guided her to a white metal bench in a shady spot of the garden. The sun and clouds jockeyed for a place in the late afternoon sky. Chanyn sank onto the bench and rubbed her neck. Khial rolled his shoulders round.

"I'm sorry," she said. "You're a bit taller than me. It was a little awkward holding your arm like that."

"I thought that's how ladies and gentlemen walked," he said. "Arms out at odd angles like that?"

A light rumble of laughter shook Chanyn's chest, bringing the outline of her nipples into view.

"Let's make a promise," she said. "Let's not do things because we think it's what we should be doing. Let's do them because we want to do them. And let's teach our child to do the same. Deal?" She put out her hand. The motion pushed her breasts together so that they swelled above the neckline of her dress.

Khial touched her hand briefly. "Deal." He sat down, his arm stretching along the back of the bench. The indent of her shoulder pressed into his side. He'd sat just like this with Dain an innumerable amount of times. The rightness of the intimate position unsettled him.

Chanyn's hand grasped her belly. She inhaled sharply, and her body jerked.

Ice skittered down Khial's spine. He sat up, rigid, unsure. He looked to her lap for any sign of blood. There was none. Chanyn sat still, eyes closed, cheeks puffed, holding her breath. Khial's hands braced in front and behind her, not sure if he should be prepared to lay her down or scoop her up.

Finally, she inhaled slowly. "It passed."

When she saw the stricken look on his face she grimaced in apology.

"Khial, it's called morning sickness. Merlyn says it lasts a few weeks at most. And that it's a good sign."

Khial nodded stiffly. He knew all these things, but he couldn't help the little voice inside his mind, the voice that called to him in nightmares and memories. The voice that wanted to poke and pop anything Khial became attached to.

He retracted his arm from behind Chanyn and folded his hand in his lap. They sat there quietly for a long moment, looking out over the lush garden. Darlyn, Dain's mother, had been full of so much love and she gave it freely, to people and plants alike. It didn't surprise Khial that the garden continued to be lush long after her passing. He wished he had an ounce of that feeling to share with this child and its mother.

"I was serious last night Khial. I don't expect anything... husbandly from you."

Khial's lips upticked at the word husbandly.

"Don't make fun." She bumped his shoulder with hers. "You're as clueless as I am about all this."

He looked over at her; the bark of laughter got stuck in his throat. With the sun backlighting her brown face and liquid eyes, Chanyn took his breath. She brought the plump lower lip into her mouth, pulling it with one tooth. Khial's mouth watered. He saw Chanyn's eyes flare.

"Khi?" She placed a hand in the crook of his elbow.

Khial's dick jerked to attention. The sudden rise after days of dormancy proved more painful than pleasurable.

He stood. "I'm going out."

Her face looked horror stricken.

Khial held up his hands as though he could stop her assumption. "Just for a while. I won't do that again, Chanyn. I promised."

The look of horror was slow to melt away. "You'll be back by dinner?"

He nodded.

She stood and held out her hand with her smallest finger extended. "Pinky swear."

"What?"

"It's something I read in a book. If you break a pinky swear, your little finger will fall off."

Khial extended his finger and linked it with hers. They shook on it, both grinning like schoolgirls. With their fingers still entwined, Khial leaned down and kissed Chanyn on the cheek. His lips tingled on contact. When he pulled back he paused for the slightest second, an inch from her mouth, before putting a breath of distance between them.

"Now you know I've told the truth," he said. "If I lose my pinky finger I won't be able to play the violin any longer."

She released his finger. Khial turned and left.

It took him twenty minutes of driving to realize where he was headed.

In Khial's worst nightmares, people looked at him with accusing eyes, even though he'd walked away from his mother all those years ago. Now, in reality, people looked at him as he walked toward her.

"She's had no visitors," the guard said in answer to Khial's question.

"None?" He'd always assumed his mother's followers, deranged men who paid homage to her work or her lineage, had been visiting her for years. They had to have done so in order to carry out the assassination of Dain's parents. An assassination Khial believed was called out due to his defection from her household.

The guard shook his head. "Not once in the ten years she's been here."

The guard had to wave Khial ahead twice. He stood, stuck in place. Khial walked slowly into the interior of the prison. He heard her before he saw her. He stopped to listen.

She breezed through the song, a song he still fumbled. The place where he always tripped up, she sailed through effortlessly. When that song ended, she immediately began another, more difficult than the first.

Khial crept to her door slowly, as though sneaking up on an opponent in a gunfight from a Western film of the twentieth. It took him five breaths before he gathered the courage to peer inside the cell door.

The woman in the room playing the violin looked nothing like the memories he lugged around of his mother. She was wrinkled and gray. Her brown skin looked sallow and unhealthy. Her hair a riot of curls upon her head. She looked... helpless.

"We do the best we can," the guard said. "But she doesn't speak and she often gets violent. You can try and talk to her if you like."

Khial shook his head. He couldn't form a sentence even if he wanted to speak with her. There was too much chatter in his head. If she'd had no visitors, then who could have caused the accident of Dain's parents? If there was no one to listen to her, who hid the cure to Dain's illness? If there was no one to follow her, whom did Khial have to guard Chanyn and the baby against?

His mother stopped playing abruptly. Slowly, as though she could sense him, she began to turn towards the door. Khial caught a glimpse of her eyes, the same crystal blue as his own, the same vacant void as the day he was born.

Khial yanked away before she could glimpse him. He walked quickly back down the hall and out the door. Never looking back, once.

CHAPTER FIVE

CHANYN DUG HER HANDS INTO the cool earth. She didn't recognize the weed she displaced. Somehow, the scrawny plant found its way amidst the lush flowers that blocked its kin from the sun. The robust flowers dwarfed and shadowed the wayward weed, but it only stretched its brown leaves higher towards the sun.

Chanyn reached for a clay pot. She filled the pot with fresh soil. Reaching for the weed, she pushed its roots into its new home and set the plant in the direct sunlight.

"What are you doing?" Khial's form blocked out the sun. A scowl darkened his features further.

Chanyn swooped the potted plant into her arms. "Was it important? Should I not have pulled this one?"

Khial barely glanced at the plant as he helped her to her feet. "Chanyn we have servants to do this. You don't have to work. You don't have to do anything."

"I like gardening. It's peaceful, especially in an area where I won't run into wild animals trying to steal my dinner or my life."

Khial sighed, releasing his scowl. "I don't want you to over exert yourself." He gave her still flat belly a fleeting look. "Please?"

The please unfolded Chanyn's arms. She kept forgetting that she had dominion over all and everyone in this house. Khial had no power or right to make her do anything. Everything he asked of her would be a request, a request she had the right to deny.

She handed the plant to Khial who set it back in the sun. Then she let him guide her into the house. Once inside, he brought her to the sink and washed her hands. She'd seen him tune his instrument one morning. He adjusted each string, one by one, with such care and focus.

One by one, Khial washed the soil from each of Chanyn's fingers.

Chanyn gazed at the concentration set in his strong jaw. His eyes were screwed in scrutiny. His tongue sneaked out of his mouth as his focus increased. Chanyn forgot to blink as she watched his every move, wondering if this is what he looked like as a boy. Would their son make that same face?

She blinked.

They wouldn't be having children. Not of their own flesh, made together. Khial didn't look at her like that, and she should be glad he didn't. She loved another man. A man she couldn't have. A man who, after coming to her aid, left without a word. Jian's priorities were crystal clear.

"What is it?" Khial stopped the water and dried her hands. "Did I hurt you?" His face screwed as he looked for damage.

"No, Khial. I was just…"

Khial tossed the towel into the sink. "You were thinking about him?"

"Dain?"

"No, the monk. Jian."

Khial put his hand on her lower back and walked her down the hallway. Chanyn forgot to speak as she concentrated on that hand at her lower back. The warmth of it. The weight of it.

"I wish things could have been different for both of us, Chanyn. But I'm learning we can't change the past. Sometimes we can't even see the past clearly for what it was."

They entered Dain's office. Chanyn sat once more on the dainty couch where Dain had proposed.

"My fathers would've done anything for my mother. They did... they did horrible things to prove their affection. Growing up, that was my definition of love. I've been so afraid of being like my parents all my life. My choices were emotion-less, like my mother, or obsessive, like my fathers. I'm still learning that I get to choose who I want to be. Dain..."

Khial stumbled, his eyes fixed on a portrait of a young Dain on the wall. In the picture, Dain looked healthy and happy, his golden locks shining around his handsome face.

"Dain would have never asked me to harm anyone. It wasn't in his nature. He only ever asked me to show others mercy or kindness. The last thing he asked me to do was take care of you and the baby. When you got sick earlier, it scared me. Everything I ever came to care about has been taken from me."

Chanyn ran her hand down his cheek. Khial shuddered, closing his eyes for a moment, as though willing himself to be still and receive the affection. Chanyn nearly pulled her hand away, but decided to keep it there.

When Khial opened his eyes, they burned into hers. "I wanted you that first day we met you. Other than Dain, I hadn't wanted something for myself in so long, and I thought you were going to try and take him from me."

Chanyn smoothed her thumb over his cheek; the coarse stubble gave her little resistance. "I just wanted to be included."

Khial covered her hand with his. "I know that now." He scooted closer and placed a hand on her cheek. "Chanyn, I... I come with a lot of baggage."

"So do I."

"I'm not a perfect man. I'm not the storybook hero like Dain."

"Yeah, I kind of figured that out," she deadpanned.

Khial froze, uncertainty on his face. Chanyn quirked an eyebrow, hoping he'd find the humor in there. It took a second, but finally a chuckle bubbled out of his chest.

He was so boyish when he laughed, when he was unguarded and forgot to shield himself from the world. Unfortunately, his shields didn't stay down for long.

Khial sobered and rebuilt his mask. But the material had grown weaker. "I'm not thoughtful like Dain. I'm not patient like Jian. I don't know that I can love you the way either of them did. But I do care about you, Chanyn. I want to provide for you, protect you, and please you."

"Okay," Chanyn said. She wanted those things, too. Not only for herself; she wanted to provide, protect, and please Khial in return. They both deserved happiness after the rough beginnings of their lives.

Khial's eyes scanned her face. Whatever he read there made him nod. "Okay," he said.

Then he leaned in, carefully, concentrating. When their lips met, it wasn't the bliss that came on Jian's breath. It wasn't the compassion that came with Dain's. Khial's kiss was his own: eager, fearful, and determined.

Chanyn relaxed into him, letting him explore her. His hands held her gently. His lips sipped at her as though she were the thing to quench the thirst within him. Khial turned her head here and there to gain maximum access. Before long Chanyn clung to him neglecting her lung's need for air.

Khial pressed her down into the couch. She felt his erection throbbing between two layers of clothing. In response, her own core heated. Chanyn became torn between pressing her legs together to relieve her ache and spreading them wide to welcome Khial.

Khial pulled away from her, breathing heavily. With shaky hands, he reached beneath her dress. Reaching her underwear, his eyes asked for permission. Chanyn gave a dazed nod and felt a tug. His knuckles brushed against her moist core and his eyes widened in surprise.

His hand shook as he relieved her of the under garment. His movements frantic, he shoved his pants down and knelt between her legs. Chanyn felt him fisting himself. He trembled as he aligned the head of his penis with her core.

He shoved into her.

Chanyn gasped. Not in pleasure. Not quite. Khial's penis was long and thick, leaving her feeling full. However, there was too much friction to enjoy the fullness.

Khial failed to notice. His face screwed in rapture as he withdrew and plunged again. And again. His pace became faster, his thrusts frantic. It became increasingly uncomfortable. Before Chanyn could decide how to voice her discomfort, it was over.

Khial shuddered inside her and slumped down into the crook of her neck. His penis softened, taking with it her discomfort. He lay atop Chanyn, his tremors subsiding, his breath unsteady, his face unguarded. A sudden protectiveness washed over Chanyn, and she stroked his neck for long moments after, as he lay there.

Finally, he straightened on his arms, a small sheepish smile on his face. Chanyn tried to return the look. Evidently, she failed.

"You... didn't?" he asked.

She searched for phrasing that wouldn't hurt his feelings.

"Did I hurt you?" Khial pulled away, his face knitting up the unguarded expression.

Chanyn fought the instinct to cover herself. Khial did it for her. He slid her dress down over her exposed thighs. Then he stood, fastening his clothing, his shield closing into place.

"Khi—" Chanyn tried to sit up, but the venture was difficult and she winced.

Khial caught sight of her expression. In one second flat his shield fell. The carefully knit expression unraveled into horror and shame.

"I'm sorry," he said. "I won't come near you again."

"Khial!"

But he was already out the door.

CHAPTER SIX

KHIAL HEARD CHANYN CALL AFTER him, but he couldn't turn back. He couldn't face her. His pride would not allow it, though his desire for her burned bright.

It was like touching a star.

Dain's words ran on a loop through Khial's head. Being inside Chanyn's wet, hot pussy had set him on fire. Khial burned to return to her and sink once more in the inferno between her thighs. He'd sated himself only moments ago, but he'd begun to grow hard again the moment he'd pulled away from her. That is, until he saw the pinched look on her face.

He raced down the hallway, putting distance between them. Ignoring Rianald's call, he burst through the front entrance and out into the cool night air.

For just a moment, I touched the Goddess.

When Dain had said that to him, Khial wondered if it was the illness talking. Now he knew from firsthand experience that the man spoke the gospel truth. Khial had no complaints about his sex life with

Dain. He'd felt fulfilled with every encounter, wanting more after each time. But being with Chanyn was something entirely different.

The moist heat of her. The soft constriction. The moist heat.

Khial's balls, emptied just moments before, felt unbearably heavy. He came to the end of the property and sat down on the curb at the main street. In the distance he could see cars carting people home after work or headed out to enjoy the city nightlife. It became a blur to Khial.

His heart ached from the loss of Dain.

His jaw throbbed from the kick delivered by that ruffian the night before in the shelter.

His head felt dizzy from the visit to his mother's cell.

And now his balls and dick wanted in on the pity party.

Khial's mind and body swirled with too much sensation. He couldn't hold on to any thought for too long. Only one thing was certain. He wanted to be back inside Chanyn.

In those few moments, he'd known peace. That same sense of peace he had after making love to Dain. In that space, when he'd pounded every ounce of pleasure from his lover and then lay in the cradle of his arms. Khial had stolen inside Chanyn, emptied his very soul into her, and known a deep sense of rightness. Only, when he opened his eyes, he found that she had experienced only discomfort and pain.

He didn't need his mother to ruin anything. He'd done a damned fine job of it himself.

When Khial was a child, peaceful moments scared him. He knew they were the calm before the storm. The only safe place in the storm of his parents lay in the eye, where he could see the fighting around him. Seeing the winds of destruction let him know which places were safe to hide. When the storm was out of sight, he felt entirely unsafe.

For the last ten years, his mother had been out of sight. Khial existed in a state of anxiety, waiting for the storm to approach. Watching for it on all fronts. Putting up shields to protect the man he loved. But that storm never came. His mother's destructive forces had been dismantled, caged, forgotten. The storm that did come hid inside Dain. Dain's illness, quiet and out of Khial's sight, blindsided him.

The first time Khial laid eyes on Dain, the boy flashed him that brilliant smile and Khial felt the ground fall out from under him. He heard the wind in his ears. He felt robbed of breath. Dain had knocked him flatter than any of the storms his parents stirred into existence. But Khial had never turned away from Dain. Never stepped out of Dain's eyesight. For years, Khial chased after the storm, until Dain's winds ceased and left Khial torn apart in the wake of its destruction.

The first time Khial saw Chanyn he felt that same prickle of wind at the nape of his neck. Everything in him told him to run. That this would be the storm to end all storms. He needed to run away from her. Run far and fast.

Khial stood and turned back to the house.

"Lord Khial?"

Khial turned at the sound of that deep, lyrical voice. The monk had the type of voice meant for singing. Once more Khial wondered what he would sound like accompanying his violin.

"Is everything all right, my lord?"

Khial thought to ask the monk the same question. Gone were his ceremonial robes of green and brown. He stood before Khial dressed in a plain cloth shirt and slacks, a back sack slung over his shoulder. The monk's broad shoulders filled out the shirt nicely and his muscled thighs rounded out the pants. Still, the clothing felt wrong in Khial's eyes. He'd seen the man entirely naked before. The splendor of his body should not be hidden under ordinary cloth.

"What are you doing here?" Khial asked.

"I was just... walking." He gazed up at the house, to the second floor. Exactly where Chanyn's bedroom sat. "Is she all right?"

"She's... She's well." Khial looked away before the monk could read the entire story of his failure in his eyes.

But then he changed his mind. "I need your help," Khial said. "With Lady Chanyn."

The monk waited. His expression, the picture of patience and non-judgment, gave nothing of his thoughts away.

Khial's lips worked soundlessly for a moment, trying to figure out the right words to explain his predicament. "I don't know what I'm doing."

The monk nodded.

"I think I may have hurt her." Khial expected to see anger on the face of the man who loved his wife. Instead, he saw expectancy, as though the monk had been waiting outside to have this very conversation.

"The first time with a woman can be a heady experience for a man. The first few times, in fact. Women are not like men. You need to make them ready."

Khial remembered the monk's instruction with Dain. That Chanyn needed to be touched before he entered her body.

"You have to take your time. Go slowly and be gentle. Their bodies cannot take the same pounding that a man's can. At least, not when they are still new to the act."

Khial also remembered that when Dain entered Chanyn's body that first time, he had been in a hurry as well. He'd gone fast and hard. And she hadn't enjoyed it.

The monk put a hand on Khial's shoulder. "Lady Chanyn is very responsive. Her body will tell you what it needs if you look and listen.

If you're still unsure, simply ask her. She's very forthcoming."

The monk gazed up at the window, a secret smile slowly spread across his face. Khial felt the monk's thumb run absently over his collar bone. Back and forth, in a hypnotic motion. Thinking about Chanyn, no doubt.

"Why don't you train me?"

The monk snapped to attention, yanking his hand away as though Khial's suggestion burned him. He took a step back, shaking his head. And then he put up his hands as though to further ward off the suggestion.

"I'll pay you."

"I don't need the money." The monk hitched his pack over his shoulder.

"You love her." Khial didn't put a question mark at the end of the statement. He knew it to be true. If he hadn't seen it in the monk's eyes, seen it in the kisses and caresses he gave Chanyn, he saw it the night before when the monk risked his own life to get Khial back to her. He saw it now, when the monk walked the city at night to gaze up at her window.

But the monk turned away from the idea.

"You love her," Khial repeated. "I don't know how to make her happy, and I want to. I don't want to hurt her. She's been through enough. We've all been through enough. We deserve a little happiness, some pleasure after the rough path of our lives. You said I could choose who I become. I choose to become a good husband to her. Teach me how to please her."

Khial knew the monk would say yes. He saw it in the give of his shoulders. He saw it as the man's head tilted up to the sky. He saw it as the monk turned weary eyes to face him.

CHAPTER SEVEN

CHANYN WOKE UP IN THE morning and began her morning ritual. She went first to the bathroom and kneeled to the porcelain goddess. Praise the Goddess, this morning her stomach decided it would keep her dinner from the previous night.

Chanyn stood and did an about face to relieve herself. She winced at the soreness between her legs. Lifting her nightdress she saw a bit of redness high up on her thighs. She sighed.

Instead of chasing after Khial last night, she'd run a bath and soaked, as Jian taught her. She hadn't needed the baths after Jian's lovemaking. The warm water and herbs helped after her tryst with Khial. The ache quieted to a dull throb. When she stood now, she barely noticed it. She wished she could run a bath strong enough to soothe Khial. She'd have to find him first. He said he wouldn't run. Part of the reason she opted for the bath last night instead of chasing after him was to learn if that promise had been the truth.

Chanyn dressed quickly. Brent and Tem were disappointed that she insisted on dressing herself, though she did allow them to shop for her and to do her hair every few days.

Chanyn made her way out of her room and down the hall. When she got to Dain's old bedroom, she knocked and waited. When there was no answer, she knocked once more and held her breath.

"He's not there."

Chanyn's heart pounded into her ears at the sound of that voice. She didn't turn around immediately. Instead, she rested her head against the bedroom door.

"He hasn't left you," the voice came closer. "He said he had an errand to run and that he'd be back shortly. Chanyn?"

A firm hand rested briefly at the small of her back before moving away quickly.

Chanyn turned slowly, and there he was. The sun shining behind him from the hall window. His bald head gleaming. His slanted eyes hooded as they gazed down at her. His lips parted in that hungry way of his.

They'd moved closer together. She, away from the door and closer to him. Him, away from the hall window and closer to her. Like magnets.

"What are you doing here?"

"I ran into Lord Khial last night."

"He came to the temple?"

Jian hesitated. "No..."

"No?"

His lips pursed. "I came here."

"Why?"

Jian sighed through his nose, his teeth grit. Then his mouth relaxed in defeat. His lips parted.

"You," he said. His hand raised and grazed her cheek. "I was walking and my feet lead me to you. I supposed I sensed you needed me, and so I came." His shrug looked like surrender. "I will always come when you call. Whether your voice or your spirit, I'll hear it and I'll be at your door."

"I don't understand? You took your vows."

"I did."

They stood without a breath between them. His legs mingling with hers. One of his hands resting at the nape of her neck, the other at the small of her back pulling her body closer.

"Lord Khial told me about last night."

Chanyn's face heated. She tried to turn away, but there was nowhere to hide.

"He asked for my help."

Chanyn turned back to Jian, wetting her lips. "You're going to help?"

His mouth ticked up in that seductive grin. "Do you want my help, my lady?"

Chanyn couldn't form words. She only nodded.

"Then, I am at your service."

"But your vow—"

"My vows do not overrule the needs of my heart." He placed his hand over her chest.

A small voice told her to take heed. There was no guarantee to the length of time he'd be here before he left again. But now, just like every other time, she couldn't stay away from him if she tried.

Chanyn reached up to pull him down. When he met her lips, there was no preamble. No sipping or tentative brushes. They delved into each other, getting lost, finding one another. It was a homecoming.

"Ahem."

Only one person would interrupt them on this floor. Chanyn slowly disentangled herself from the man she loved to face the man she'd married.

Khial walked slowly towards them, one hand shoved in his pocket, the other holding a beautifully wrapped package. Watching his powerful legs move in the light cloth of his slacks, Chanyn had trouble recalling the pain of his thrusts. She met his eyes and saw them flare. Jian released his hold on her neck.

Jian's face was impassive but she saw the telltale sign of guilt on his lowered brow. She was sure Khial saw the heat rising off her face and chest. He gave them both an awkward smile. It might have been his normal smile. Chanyn still wasn't used to anything but a scowl when he looked at her.

"Good morning," Khial said.

Jian and Chanyn murmured felicitations back to him.

"How are you feeling this morning, my lady?"

Chanyn heard the weight in the question. How badly did I hurt you? Do you hate me? Will you never let me touch you again?

She stepped toward him. "Khi, I'm fine.

He caught her hands before she could touch him, searching for the lie in those words. Finding none, he swallowed what appeared to be a huge lump caught in his throat. He loosened his grip and stepped into her. His one arm held her stiffly, but his chest felt warm, hopeful, safe.

He stepped back abruptly. "I thought we could try again. Later. With some help." He stretched his hand out to indicate Jian.

Chanyn nodded. "I'd like that."

Khial looked so alone and bereft. Much like she felt weeks ago when he and Dain found her. Her greatest desire had been to be welcomed into their bond. Khial had been hesitant with her. She didn't feel the same hesitancy with him. She wanted to share her heart with him.

Khial handed her the package. "I brought this for you."

From the weight and shape of the package, Chanyn could tell it was a book. No. A stack of books.

"They were my mother's. I have some of her things in storage. Things the Sisterhood found of no value. I thought you would like them."

Chanyn unwrapped the package to find a stack of thin Harlequin romance novels from the twentieth century.

"I used to think books like these were dangerous. That they caused women to pit men against each other. I realize it's not the book, it's the person. People choose how they receive information and what they do with that information. I trust you."

Chanyn knew that those last words were high praise from this man. "Thank you Khial. I will treasure these."

He shrugged, but she saw the relief and pride in his light eyes. Relief that she liked his gift and understood his gesture. Pride that he'd made a good decision and taken a step in the right direction.

"Anyway, I'll see you tonight." He wouldn't quite meet her eyes. He took a step around her, but Chanyn stayed him with her hand. She reached up and kissed him lightly on the lips. She felt his inhale of surprise. Then, as she stayed still a moment longer pressed against his lips, she felt him exhale and relax into her.

When she pulled away, he gave her the smallest of smiles, but it was a genuine smile, straight from the wounded organ that was his heart. His hand snaked around his head and scratched at the nape of his neck. He nodded once to her, then behind her to Jian, and walked into his bedroom shutting the door behind him.

Chanyn turned to Jian, who grinned at the closed door.

"Jian?"

He gave her his full attention.

"How long are you here this time?"

"For as long as you need me."

CHAPTER EIGHT

"MATERNAL GODDESS, I SEEK YOUR presence as I align myself with one of your sacred daughters.

I offer my body as a vessel of your will and your grace.

The desire of my heart is pure and known to you.

I wish to please your daughter and garner your favor.

The miracle that pleases a woman and creates life is of your design, Divine Goddess.

With great anticipation, I align all of the energy systems of my body, my soul, and my mind with you.

I give thanks in advance for your blessings of this experience and know that I walk in the light of your sun and the fertility of your earth.

Ashe."

The monk's melodic voice decresendoed. Again, Khial wondered how that deep tenor might sound accompanying his violin.

Jian asked for stillness. He and Chanyn closed their eyes in a silent moment of gratitude to the Goddess.

Khial picked at the buttons of his shirt, the itch on his nose. He looked around Chanyn's bedroom. Large blooms decorated a dresser near the window, beside them teetered the stack of books he'd gifted her. Golden-haired men clenching women with swollen bodices dominated each cover. Khial scratched at his chest.

The monk clasped Khial's hand. Khial's dick pulsed in time to the circular pattern the monk traced on the flesh between Khial's thumb and index finger. Was the monk trying to seduce him? Khial looked for a hint in the monk's eyes, but they remained closed.

Between them, both men held Chanyn's hands in each of their own. Her hands were by no means delicate. They were capable and strong. She interlaced two of her fingers with Khial's, leaving him feeling grounded, tethered. And aroused.

Khial tried to take his mind off his dick and focus on the two people on either side of him. Their fingers were wholly entwined. Their palms pressed together. Suddenly, Khial felt like an intruder. Chanyn and the monk loved each other and he was imposing on their intimacy.

The monk opened his eyes and focused on Khial. The monk— Jian. Khial figured he should start using his name, as they were about to be intimate. Jian's eyes said he read Khial's desire loud and clear, but he cast no judgment. Instead, a flicker of heat sparked in the other man's eyes.

Khial swallowed. It was too soon to think about another man. He was still getting used to the idea of a woman, his wife. He looked over at Chanyn.

"Should you always pray... before?" Khial directed the comment at no one in particular, but he knew who would answer.

"A woman's body is sacred," answered Jian. "If you do not prefer to pray, you should at least set an intention."

"An intention?"

Jian nodded. "Our intention tonight is to pleasure the lady." Jian turned to Chanyn. "Pleasure her until she begs for mercy."

A slow, intentional smile spread across the monk's face. He rose to his feet bringing Khial and Chanyn along.

Jian stood behind Chanyn and turned her to face Khial. She'd dressed in a simple nightgown of light purple silk. Lace ties held the flimsy garment together. Her dark nipples poked against the material.

"Undo the laces, my lord."

Khial's hands shook like the strings of his instrument. Not from nervousness—not entirely. Khial trusted Jian to make this experience pleasurable, not only for Chanyn, but for all. Khial's fingers trembled in anticipation as he lifted them to the first tie.

Chanyn smiled in encouragement as she watched Khial's progress. I trust you, that smile said. Khial felt his heart expand a fraction.

Jian also marked his progress with the ties. His dark eyes portraying the same trust. Khial was not one to trust easily. He could count on one finger the number of people he'd trusted. The idea that he trusted these two people, whom he'd known for such a short time, astounded him. The hard fact that he did trust them both steadied his fingers, and Khial pulled the last tie free.

Jian swept the garment from Chanyn's shoulders. Khial's fingers, his legs, his dick, lost the battle of steadiness. He began to throb from his eyelashes to the space between his toes. Chanyn stood completely bare before him.

Her brown breasts full, her erect nipples pebbled, so dark they appeared black. Her waist narrowed into a sculpted stomach with curves and planes. Her hips flared out to powerful thighs. A dark set of curls lay at the juncture between her thighs.

Khial's mouth watered. He'd dreamed of that space last night. Of diving in there once more. Of getting lost in the bliss of that warm heat. Of their own accord, his hands reached out, but Jian pulled her away.

Khial glared. Jian only smiled that serene smile of his station. Khial's blood heated. Was this a trick? He'd seen his fathers fighting over time in the bedroom with his mother. Her door locked while one of them banged at the exterior for entrance. Would this come to a fight?

Jian didn't look adversarial. "We need to prepare her," he said.

He guided Chanyn towards the bed. When she turned, Khial caught a glimpse of the orbs of her ass. His dick, already hard as a rock, strained painfully against his pants. Khial took a step to follow, but Jian's hand stayed him once more. Khial's glare threatened murder.

The monk, placid as ever, said, "Breathe."

Khial clenched his teeth.

Jian released Chanyn and brought both hands to Khial's shoulders. Khial's instinct was to shove him off. Jian's thumbs rubbed circles at a point on Khial's shoulders and, like magic, the aggression seeped out of Khial.

"I need you to be present, my lord," Jian said quietly, for Khial's ears only. "I need you to have a clear head. We are going to please her first."

The emphasis on her snapped the fog from Khial's mind. A front of shame moved in. He'd gone to Jian for help in making the act pleasurable for Chanyn. In the first minute, he'd let his Neanderthal instincts overpower him.

Jian tilted Khial's head up so that they looked each other in the eye. Khial wondered how this man could allow him access to the woman he so clearly worshipped. But the woman the monk worshipped was Khial's wife, now. Khial allowed Jian access to her. Once more, Khial felt Jian read his mind because what he saw reflected in the monk's dark eyes was gratitude.

Khial leaned into Jian's touch, grateful for the support. He wanted to rest in Jian's embrace for a moment longer, but Jian gave his shoulders a final squeeze and then he turned them both towards Chanyn. She lay on the bed like an offering.

Khial came before the bed and kneeled. Jian went to the other side.

Jian ran his hand over Chanyn's face. It was a move Dain had done to Khial countless times. It signified love and trust. Chanyn closed her eyes, her entire body going to another level of relaxation.

"With men, we need very little preparation other than a wink and a nod," Jian said, a smile in his voice. He nodded at Khial to mimic his motions on Chanyn's body. Khial slowly raised his hands. They shook once more as they hovered over Chanyn.

"Women's bodies are different," Jian continued his lesson. "That tremble in their bodies means that they are mentally open to intimacy. It takes a moment for their pleasure centers to awaken."

Jian's hands moved lightly over Chanyn's body. His fingertips danced across the planes of her body, around the mounds of her breasts, over the peaks of her nipples, up to the hollow of her throat, down into the valley between her thighs.

Khial felt a hand on his own. Chanyn gazed at him, kindness crinkled the corners of her eyes. Khial felt the cage around his heart fracture. Chanyn pulled his hand to her chest. He felt her strong heartbeat. The strength of it scared him. She moved his hand from her heart and brought it to her lips, kissing his fingers lightly. Trust mingled with desire in that smile. She left his hand on her breast and then closed her eyes once more.

Khial's hands traveled the mound and peaks of Chanyn's breasts. Chanyn parted her lips and sighed.

"Very good, Lord Khial. Watch for her responses. Her body will tell you what is pleasing, if you look for the signs."

Khial saw the signs instantly. When he touched her lightly, she trembled, arching up into his hands. When he firmed his touch, her lower body ground into the mattress seeking traction. She was an instrument, her limbs the chords. Khial played her, learning the keys to her melodies.

Jian sat back on his heels and watched Khial's ministrations, a smile of satisfaction on his face. That look of satisfaction made Khial prideful. He'd never been great at school, outside of music. Teachers usually looked at him with disdain. Khial couldn't muster the inclination to care. As a first born and royal, he would never need to do much with his brain. Watching the pride in the monk's eyes made Khial want to ace this examination.

The monk's smile did spread. In mischief. "Excellent job with your hands, my lord. Now, we'll use our mouths."

Both Khial and Chanyn's bodies shuddered. Jian leaned over Chanyn's body, closer to Khial. The monk's hand filled with one of Chanyn's breasts.

"I want you to determine which she likes most." Jian curled his tongue and flicked it lightly over Chanyn's nipple. "A light touch?"

Chanyn's body undulated.

Jian's tongue flattened and traced another trail. "A firm touch?"

Khial leaned into the side of the bed to give his dick some much needed friction.

"Or a bite." Jian's teeth clamped lightly around Chanyn's nipple. Her eyelids strained to her brow. Jian ran a gentle hand down the side of her face. "And remember," he said to Khial, "our intention is to make her beg for mercy."

A look of stubbornness settled over Chanyn's features. The look told them she accepted the challenge, and wouldn't be so easily won.

A smirk lit Jian's face. "You will see, my lord, that the bedroom is the only place where a man has the opportunity to rule a woman."

The monk moved to the base of the bed and settled between Chanyn's thighs. He spread Chanyn's legs wide, then stretched himself out and rested his head on the inside of one thigh as though he planned to stay for a long while.

"Go on, then," Jian nodded to her breast.

Chanyn's eyes narrowed on Khial in challenge. They were on opposite teams. He'd watched her play card games with Dain. Dain was notorious at card games. He loved to win. Khial had never been very competitive. Whenever Dain moved in to make the killer play, he got this look of challenge in his eyes. That was the look in Chanyn's eyes. And suddenly Khial wanted very much to win.

Game on.

Khial lowered his head and did as Jian instructed. Softly, he traced the underside of Chanyn's breasts. The crease of the skin at the base of the mound intrigued him. Chanyn gasped, showing her hand, then clamped her mouth shut. Khial chuckled and played his next move.

With a firm flick of his tongue, he traced from that bottom crease to the peak of her breast. Chanyn rested a trembling hand on his shoulder, panting, but still she kept all words from her mouth, determined to stay in the game. Khial made a show of baring his teeth. Her breaths kicked up.

She was going to lose.

He bit down lightly. Chanyn's nails dug into his shoulder. Khial wrapped his entire mouth around the top of her breast and suckled. He moaned, himself, at the taste and feel of her. Her hands moved from his shoulder and into his hair. She cradled his neck as he continued to suckle. Khial became lost, but not for long. He remembered Jian's words.

I need you to have a clear head.

Khial released Chanyn's breast with a pop. Her eyes remained closed in absolute bliss. Pride shot through him at the sight. The restrictions around his heart relaxed. He caught Jian's nod of approval before the monk dipped his head between Chanyn's thighs. Khial watched, transfixed, as Jian ran his tongue lightly at the pink opening between Chanyn's thighs. Her deep moan brought Khial's attention back to her face. Her eyes screwed shut, her mouth wide, her chest panting.

"No mercy, my lord." Jian's lips glossed with Chanyn's juices.

Khial's mouth watered. Whether at the desire to taste Chanyn's juices, or to taste Jian's lips, or both.

Jian grinned, a kid at a berry stand, then he inclined his head towards Chanyn's other breast indicating for Khial to get back to work. He disappeared between Chanyn's thighs. His mouth devoured her, his tongue flicked over the pink bud at the apex of her thighs.

Chanyn trembled—no—she shook. Her moans turned to cries of the purest ecstasy. They filled Khial's ears and settled somewhere deep inside his chest. Deep inside where his own core lay, and it warmed him through.

Like a two-piece instrument, they played her. Jian's tongue stroked her firmly, Chanyn ground her hips. Khial nibbled at her breasts lightly, the upper half of her body arched toward him. The opposing touches drove her to madness.

Khial had never been interested in power. He had no desire to rule Chanyn. But he did relish the command he had over her body. It was like the first time he picked up the violin. It had called to him, begged him to uncover its mysteries. To practice until he'd mastered it. That's how he felt now, with Chanyn in his hands.

Her moans were guttural, animal. Her body jerked out of control. She was climaxing, Khial realized. He released her breasts and watched.

Chanyn dug her heels into the bed, her fists tangled in the sheets. Her entire body moved in a wave, like the tide crashing into the shore, over and over again.

When the waves receded, Jian moved alongside her. The monk wrapped his arms about Chanyn and held her tight, murmuring nonsensical words of love to her temple. He smiled over at Khial. Job well done, that look said.

Disappointment washed through Khial. He was nowhere near finished playing.

Jian chuckled. "Take off your pants, my lord."

Khial blinked. The monk raised an eyebrow and waited patiently for Khial to follow his instruction. Khial stood on shaky legs. What would happen now? Chanyn looked done for the night. He assumed any minute she'd roll over and fall asleep. What then? Would Jian relieve him? Did Khial want that?

Khial slowly unbuckled his pants and let them fall to the ground. Jian watched the motion, his hand stroking Chanyn's back, easing her quakes to light trembles. Jian reached over to the side table and grabbed a circular device. He handed it to Khial. Electricity tingled Khial's palm as Jian's fingers skittered over his. When Khial looked down, he recognized the device.

"You want me to wear this?" he asked the monk.

The monk placed a light kiss on Chanyn's temple, never taking his eyes off Khial. "Trust me."

Again, something shifted in Khial's chest when he realized that he did. Not only did he trust the monk, he wanted to please the monk. He'd never cared to please anyone but Dain. Khial clamped the conception ring around the base of his dick, then looked to Jian for further instruction.

Khial's dick throbbed as the monk sat up. But the monk brought Chanyn with him. Jian sat with his back against the headboard. He turned Chanyn so that she lay on his chest. Then he reached down her body and brought her knees to a kneeling position around his torso. In that position, Khial realized Jian meant for him to take Chanyn from behind.

"Women can orgasm many times a night, with little to no break in between."

Jian motioned for Khial to place himself behind Chanyn. Khial's hands began to shake once more. He remembered being buried in that damp, tight space. The warmth of it, the tightness. He tried to breathe through his eagerness to return. After witnessing Chanyn in pleasure, he never wanted their coupling to cause her pain again. He wanted to give her the bliss she was in now.

"Don't worry. She's ready for you. You will not hurt her."

Chanyn's head rested against Jian's chest. Jian traced a lazy pattern on her spine as he watched Khial.

Khial spread his thighs wide on the outside of both Jian's and Chanyn's legs. He lined himself against Chanyn's wet heat. Slowly, had been Jian's instruction to Dain. Gritting his teeth, Khial entered her slowly.

In his mind's eye, he saw paradise. He felt peace. Seated fully in her, his balls ached for immediate release, but the device wouldn't allow it.

Chanyn's moan brought him back to this plane of existence. Her eyes remained closed as she clung to Jian. Her lower body arched back into Khial. Slowly, Khial began to move. Chanyn met him thrust for thrust. His hands rested lightly against her hips. They tightened with each thrust.

Jian reached up and took one of Khial's hands. The monk pulled Khial's hand around and rested it on the bud between Chanyn's thighs. She moaned deeper, back caving in.

"Circles. Slow, but firm," Jian instructed.

Khial did as he was told. Chanyn used her hands to push away from

Jian's chest. Jian let her go. Ecstasy written on his face as he watched.

Chanyn's arms curled around Khial's neck. Her face against his cheek. "Khi," she whispered.

Khial pulled her back flush against his chest. Though he wanted to go faster, harder, he kept his thrusts steady, the circles slow and firm. And soon she was quaking. Her body jerked and convulsed around his.

"Khial," she shouted.

Khial saw stars as that warm wet heat he craved caved in on him. His balls seized, but couldn't release. He couldn't hold on to reality. Chanyn fell out of his arms, and into Jian's waiting embrace. Jian held her with one arm and reached the other out to Khial. He cupped Khial's face, his fingers extending to the back of his neck. Khial closed his eyes and welcomed the strong, steady embrace.

They stayed like that for Goddess knew how long. And then Khial felt warm fingers on his dick. He looked down to see Jian's fingers releasing the ring.

His eyes bored into Khial's. There were so many emotions there: desire, trust, awe, peace.

The convulsions of Chanyn's orgasm nearly shoved him out of her, but the tip of Khial's dick remained stubbornly inside her. Khial watched as Jian gathered the woman he loved into his arms and set his mouth to hers. Chanyn still trembled, but she relaxed into Jian's kisses. Khial watched them until he was distracted by the throbbing of his dick. He looked down at it. Chanyn writhed against it under Jian's ministrations. Khial caught Jian's eyes. Never breaking from Chanyn's lips, the monk nodded once at Khial.

Khial pushed himself back inside. Chanyn's entire being shook. Jian held her firm. Khial closed his eyes and tried to go slow.

"She can take it harder now," Jian said.

Khial opened his eyes to make sure it hadn't been his own desire speaking. It hadn't. Jian nodded at him in confirmation. Khial thrust upward a little harder. Chanyn gasped, but it was a gasp he'd come to know. The gasp that said she was pleased and near her own release. And so he did it again. Chanyn's body, which had just been wracked by a second climax only moments ago, tensed around him. He thrust again, and then again.

Jian continued kissing and petting her, whispering words of love. Words that Khial closed his eyes and allowed to penetrate his mind, his aching heart. Khial reached between them and put one hand on her breasts, the other on her hip and thrust even deeper. One of Chanyn's arms wrapped once more around his neck. A hand grasped his ass.

He knew that hand wasn't Chanyn's. It urged him on faster, harder. Trust me, that hand said. You won't hurt her, it assured him.

Khial trusted the hand and thrust harder and faster. He heard the sound of Jian's lips against her mouth as she gasped, moaned, and cried. He heard the sound of his body slapping against Chanyn's ass. The heat poured through every crevice of his body, loosening the spots that had gone cold and dark since Dain's passing. Khial opened.

"Mercy," Chanyn cried out and convulsed around him.

His balls could take no more and they burst forth, emptying into her. He thrust and thrust until everything in him released into her. He thrust one more time to make sure he'd left nothing behind. He was done. Undone. Remade.

As if choreographed, Khial collapsed to one side of Chanyn, Jian to the other. They lay there in a cocoon of peace. Warmth flooded his body, his being. Peace in his mind.

Like touching the Goddess.

He swore he felt Dain at his back whispering for him to fall asleep. That he had him, always.

Chanyn lay in the spoon of Jian's arms. Jian's head rested against Khial's forearm just above Chanyn's. Chanyn's head rested over Khial's heart.

Khial kept his eyes open and on the scene for as long as he could. He felt the instinct to protect those in his care. But for the first time in days, he felt safe and warm. He scooted closer to Chanyn. Somehow, his free hand found Jian's hip. Enclosed in the circle, Khial allowed himself to be lulled to sleep.

CHAPTER NINE

JIAN LEANED FORWARD, CLOSER TO the two sleeping individuals beside him. His heart sighed at the sight of Chanyn's tranquil face. Over her shoulder, Lord Khial's body sank deeply into the mattress. Last night, the young man stressed over every touch with Chanyn, afraid he'd hurt her. Now his hand twined with hers, curled over her belly.

All day, Jian watched the man hide his growing feelings for Chanyn behind his sense of duty, insisting his every move was for her benefit and not the growing feelings he had for her. Lord Khial was intensely loyal and determined. Jian could not have asked for a better man to be paired with the woman he loved.

Jian slid his fingertips down Chanyn's cheek. She would be okay without him. And that time was approaching. Jian rose from the bed. His motions caused Chanyn to sigh and roll forward, but she continued to slumber peacefully.

Lord Khial opened his eyes. "Are you leaving?"

Jian paused, his gaze raking over Lord Khial's bare chest. "I wouldn't leave her without saying goodbye. I'm just going for a walk."

Lord Khial sat up slowly, also trying to avoid waking Chanyn. "Would you join me for first meal?"

Jian nodded.

The two men dressed quietly. Once or twice Jian caught the lord sneaking a look at his chest as he buttoned up the cloth shirt. Jian's eyes dipped once or twice, as Lord Khial fumbled at his pants. Lord Khial opened the door for Jian. They made their way down the stairs side by side. Occasionally a knuckle brushed a hand. At the bottom of the stairs, Jian motioned for Lord Khial to precede him. Jian couldn't help but notice the strong stride of the man in front of him.

In the dining room, Rianald set a feast before them. Jian reached for the berries, then pulled back. The sweets were an indulgence. But he remembered he was no longer a monk. So he heaped them onto his plate.

"How long can you stay with us?" Lord Khial asked.

Jian wanted to stay with Chanyn forever. But that wasn't possible, regardless of his new station. Chanyn was a bonded woman. "I'll stay as long as you need me, my lord."

Lord Khial brightened at this answer. "The temple can spare you for a while?"

Jian hesitated. They would find out, sooner or later. "I've been thro—" He choked on the word. He cleared his throat and shoved the truth into the light of day. "I've been thrown out of the temple."

"Thrown out?"

"Well, not thrown, but I am unable to return."

"Since when?"

"Since the night I came for you."

"Because of me?"

Jian wobbled his head yes and no. "Because of my feelings for Lady Chanyn."

"Because you love her?"

Jian gave a firm nod, then popped another cherry into his mouth.

"So, you're a free man?"

Jian hadn't thought of it that way. He'd thought only in the negative. He wasn't a monk. "Yes. It would appear that I am."

A free man. A third son. Discarded three times now.

"What will you do?"

Jian frowned, his brows furrowed. He would have to find some employment. The best situation would likely be as a manservant. Ideally, he would've loved to work for this house and keep an eye on Chanyn. But he would eventually wind up putting more than an eye on her. He respected Lord Khial too much to betray him in such away.

"I'd like you to stay," Lord Khial said.

"I can't. I can't be this close to her and not keep my hands off her."

"Then don't keep your hands off her."

Jian's mouth fell open.

"You could bond with us."

Jian chomped down on the berry in his mouth. The fruit, sweeter than he expected, caused him to wince. Lord Khial's words didn't make sense, so Jian spouted what he knew to be true.

"You can't mean that. It's the orgasms talking. You should never make decisions so close after sex."

"Fine," Lord Khial said.

Jian's heart stalled at the quick withdrawal.

"Stay a few days, and then I'll ask you again."

Jian blinked. "You can't possibly want me."

Lord Khial didn't meet Jian's eyes. "Lady Chanyn wants you. And Dain wanted me to keep her happy."

It was the same logic Lord Khial'd given Jian about not hurting Chanyn. Lord Dain, and not himself, would be upset if Chanyn were hurt. Jian saw right through it, but he still couldn't quite make himself believe it.

"I'm a third. A discard. All the scandal—"

Lord Khial laughed. This time he did meet Jian's eyes. "This house is full of scandal." Lord Khial looked around, as though it were his first time in the room. "It's also the happiest home in the city. I think you'd do well as a part of it."

Lord Khial held Jian's glance. The glance was unmistakable. Jian had had love affairs with men before. He knew the look of a man who desired him. The other night, as Lord Khial thrust into Chanyn, Jian imagined the man driving into him. With Chanyn in his arms and Lord Khial moving above him, Jian had nearly climaxed.

Lord Khial must have read Jian's thoughts. His blue eyes widened, his nostrils flared. But he looked away, shame tinting the edges of his eyes. Lord Khial wanted that scene too, but Jian knew it would be some time before he might actually consider acting on it. The loss of Lord Dain still hung heavily in this house and in Lord Khial's heart.

"I am not what happens to me. I choose who I become." Lord Khial's clear blue eyes met Jian's. "You taught me that."

Before Jian could respond, the manservant, Rianald approached.

"Brother Jian, there is a Brother Gerry here to see you. He would not come inside. So, I escorted him to the gardens."

What was Elder Gerry doing here? Was there some emergency at the temple? Or... Jian hesitated to think it. Had he come to offer Jian his robes back? To welcome him back home?

Jian looked to Lord Khial who watched him, clearly wondering the same.

"Would you excuse me a moment, my lord?"

Lord Khial nodded. Jian rose, but then hesitated, his body wedged between two different worlds. Slowly, he turned and headed out the door to the gardens.

Elder Gerry stood admiring the lush blooms, a serene smile on his face. The old man turned at Jian's approach.

"And so, we meet in a garden instead of a field." Elder Gerry said by way of greeting.

It took Jian a moment to understand the reference. The last time they spoke, the older man talked of an ancient koan where individuals would meet in a field passed wrongs and rights. Koans didn't have concrete meanings. You were supposed to sit and think on them at length, potentially for a lifetime.

Jian had no patience for riddles, at the moment. "What brings you here, Elder Gerry?"

Elder Gerry must've heard the impatience in Jian's voice, because he got down to the point. "I come seeking your help, my friend."

Not son. Not brother.

"Whatever I can do, you know I will."

"Your success continues to bear us fruits."

"My success?"

"With Lady Chanyn. Word spread that she conceived a girl child on the first try and then conceived again shortly after her loss. Families of a few young girls are requesting our services as their young daughters approach marriageable age in the next few years."

"What are you asking me? To rejoin the temple?"

"No. I am not asking you to don the robes once more. Your heart is fully entrenched outside of the temple." He looked back to the house. "But, we need to recruit and train new brothers."

New brothers. It was what Jian had been hoping for, for years. Fresh recruits to replenish the ranks. But their reputation had been so dismal, their finances so negligible that not even street thirds saw them as a viable career opportunity.

"The brothers and I discussed it. We'd like you to work for the temple as a teacher. To train the next generation."

"A teacher? Not a brother?"

"A teacher has access to the temple, but outside of the temple, the temple does not have access to the teacher. The teacher would be free to love whom they chose. It seemed the best way through, to me."

Glancing back at the house, Jian saw Lord Khial watching them from the window. Lady Chanyn walked up behind him, her hand on her belly. She reached up to her husband and spoke. In answer, Lord Khial pointed out the window. Chanyn's face brightened when she saw Jian. She leaned in to her husband and smiled at her lover.

Jian looked back at the man who'd veritably raised him. The man who'd rescued him after being discarded. He opened his mouth and gave Elder Gerry the only answer he could.

CHAPTER TEN

CHANYN STOOD AT THE SHELF and watched as the two figures ran their hands over her wardrobe. Her heart pounded rapid fire, like the percussion of a woodpecker's beak. She glanced up at what opportunity brought to her door.

"Are you ready?"

Khial framed the entrance to her bedroom where Tem and Brent fussed over the final touches to Chanyn's dress. He was splendid in a beige suit. His brown skin like the fertile earth, his blue eyes a clear sky. A small smile played on his lips. It quivered like the smallest string on his violin.

Khial offered his arm. Chanyn put her hand in the crook, tucked safe and secure. They crossed the threshold together and headed towards the stairs.

"Are you sure about this?" she asked.

"You don't...?" Khial tensed the muscles of his bicep, trapping her fingers.

"No, no. I do."

Khial relaxed his arm. "Good." But then he frowned. "I just realized I never asked you if this is what you wanted to do. I just assumed. Dain and I knew each other for so long, we just always assumed what the other wanted. And in the times we were wrong..." He smiled that secret smile when he thought of the good times with Dain. "The times we were wrong, we spent convincing each other of the rightness of our positions."

He shared that secret smile with her. He'd begun doing that more often. Sharing stories of Dain along with small smiles.

"My assumption is right, though?" he said. "You do want to bond with Jian. You love him." It wasn't a question. Khial stated the facts.

"I do." Chanyn tucked her free arm around his bicep, lacing her fingers. She leaned her head against his arm. She loved Khial, too. Not in the same heady, romantic way she loved Jian. Not in the same steady, companionable way she loved Dain. When Chanyn looked at Khial, she saw herself, a lonely person reaching out. Chanyn grasped Khial's arm tighter, squeezing herself into his side. Trying to let him know that she was there, that she would always be there for him, holding his hand and his heart.

"I want that for you," Khial put his hand over hers. "For you to have the man you love, in your life." Absentmindedly, he rubbed her fingers, particularly her ring finger which carried the gem of himself and Dain. A fourth gem joined the three. Jian's; a green malachite, which symbolized healing. "I trust him, and I respect him. Jian is loyal."

At the bottom of the staircase stood the man in question. Jian waited for them, dressed in the same beige ceremonial clothes as Khial. His gold sash tied around his waist. Though he no longer wore his robes, he kept his sash. It represented the knowledge he'd earned from his time at the temple. That would never be taken from him. It was that knowledge the monks now sought from him. In a month, Jian would begin training a new class of Pleasure Hounds.

Chanyn watched as Jian took in Khial, the same heat mirrored in the eyes of both males. Then Jian's eyes fell to Chanyn. His face lit with delight. Chanyn felt her entire body warm. The warmth traveled from her heart to her stomach. She knew it was too soon but she was sure she felt a kick in her gut.

Khial squeezed her hand and led them both down the stairs to Jian. The room below was filled with the people who cared about them. The manservants, Rianald, Tem, and Brent stood off to the side. Merlyn, and her intended bond mate stood together. And throughout the room stood the monks of Jian's temple, all come to celebrate their brother.

A month ago, Chanyn had been alone, wishing for family and love. She had Khial's hand in one. With the other hand she took Jian's. In her belly, growing stronger every day, was the love she shared with Dain. Chanyn had yearned all her life for her one true love. In the end, she had found three.

Hand in hand, the three of them walked forward to say the vows that would link them together for the rest of their lives.

ACKNOWLEDGEMENTS

This book would not have happened without my Dynamos! Leslye, Kara and Angela.

I also have to thank my amazing Street Team: Michelle C., Michelle D., Ella, and Tina.

And a huge shout-out to the Self Publishing Yahoo Group who led me away from making so many missteps in my foray into self-publishing.

In case you're interested in where the title The Pleasure Hound came from, here's the story. I was up one night watching HBO's After Dark programing. On a show called Cathouse, one of the 'working girls' captivated me. She looked like a kindergarten teacher, not anything like what I'd imagine a hooker to look like. She said that she was a "pleasure hound;" that she could sniff out pleasure wherever it might be. The phrase stuck in my head for years. So when Jian appeared in my head, removed his hood, and asked how he could please me, I knew exactly what to call him.

Ines Johnson
Erotica, Paranormal, and Fairytales -Oh my!

If you LIKE me my heart will TWITTER!

 @ineswrites

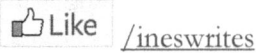 /ineswrites

 inesjohnson.wordpress.com

www.ingramcontent.com/pod-product-compliance
Lightning Source LLC
Chambersburg PA
CBHW072210170626
46813CB00003B/867